the ruin of the watcher
fox argall mysteries
book one

Collings MacCrae

The Collings Group

Copyright © 2022 by Lisa Blanton dba Collings MacCrae and The Collings Group

All rights reserved.

No part of this book may be reproduced in any form or by any electronic or mechanical means, including information storage and retrieval systems, without written permission from the author, except for the use of brief quotations in a book review.

This book was originally published on Kindle Vella.

This is a work of fiction flowing directly from my wrought imagination. It depicts no person alive or dead. No part of this book, including original art, may be reproduced in any form that exists now or in the future, or by any electronic or mechanical means, including information storage and retrieval systems, without written permission from the author, except for the use of brief quotations in a book review.

This book was originally published in part on Amazon's Kindle Vella platform in episodes. This 4th edition version is expanded from the Vella version.

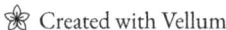 Created with Vellum

foreword

The Ruin of the Watcher is book one in Fox Argall Mysteries. It tells Fox's story from the age of fifteen through the horror that leads him to police work. The books can be read stand-alone, but the foundation begins here.

Ellis 'Fox' Argall, MD, PhD, JD is the star of the show, but his neurospecial life requires an ensemble cast of main characters that build a support framework around him. In the e-book versions, find this indispensable team and their roles in the *Main Series Cast of Characters*. Each book introduces a new group of antagonists and secondary characters that bring color to the case at hand. Some of them stick around, for good and for bad.

Each e-book has a linked *Table of Contents*.
Thanks for reading my books!

prologue

DARKNESS

The dragging sound could have alerted someone other than fleeing wildlife, had anyone been awake. But no one was.

The rustling might have been heard from the short distance to either road. The moans would surely have brought helping hands and deliverance. But there were no ears to hear.

The scuffling began when that small soul awoke and took its stand. Had help been near, there may have been a different reality. A different present. Surely, a different future. But the spirit proved too faint for the battle, and soon the darkness fell again.

one
evening—the first day

GRACE SITS IN TWILIGHT. The room glows orangey-pink from the makeup mirror, reflecting wasted attempts to tame her red curls into something beyond a damp tangle. She wears a baggy, old Fox tee that should have been tossed, but she can't resist the soft, tissue-like texture. Undergarments slide and creep and pinch and choke these days.

Who knew middle-aged ladies walk around naked underneath?

"Who are you?" she says aloud, staring at herself in the mirror. Estrogen is fading from her like a blind closing off light, pulling at her skin.

My body is drying up. Thoughts swirl in her head, unbidden, as her foundation cracks.

Grace's husband watches her from the doorway. "Your stunning breasts," Fox murmurs in his low rumble.

She shivers, her body reacting to a sudden chill. The dim room hides her response. *I should sit in the dark more often. I need space these days. Space to figure out who I'm becoming.*

Fox leans against the door frame, his shirttail out of his pants, tie loose.

Trousers, Grace reminds herself. Her Welshman husband always corrects her in his fancy accent: 'Pants are undergarments.'

Like the ones I'm not wearing.
Ellis Cadnon 'Fox' Argall. Her husband doesn't move like ordinary men. He's feline, muscles coiled, moving with a predator's intense elegance. Reincarnation pops into Grace's thoughts. *Fox would be a cat—a black leopard, stalking, muscles and sinews rippling.*

His eyes are light olive green with those maddening black lashes—the kind men grow and women envy. Fox grazes upon Grace in an unsettling way, absorbing her.

I lose myself. I can't resist him, even now.

Disconnected, her meandering thoughts sound like those women's books with long-haired men on the covers.

Grace smiles at her husband through the mirror's protection, her irritation growing as she pretends poise. She wants to hide. Instead, she laughs, the sound harsh to her ears.

"The lady loves the compliment, rogue. She's up here." Grace spins on the stool, pointing to her face. The shadows mask her fiery, unstoppable blush. She remembers she's irritated, but she can't explain why.

"I love your sweet face too," Fox purrs, and she can hear his beautiful eyes twinkling.

Demanding eyes. Relentless, claiming her. Overwhelming her. Lately, it all just pisses her off.

Her visceral annoyance at his intensity reminds her of Groucho Marx. *I wouldn't want to be a member of a club that would have me.*

Fox's need for Grace is one she's never sure she can meet. She's less sure today than during their thirty years together.

Age is a thief. What has time stolen from Fox? Nothing. And that pisses her off, too.

Fox is tall. He appears thin until you notice he isn't thin at all. Lithe, like a linebacker whose size surprises you. He was so pretty when he was younger and looked like a girl.

Not anymore.

Eventually, his face chiseled up. Small lines deepened around those eyes and his strong mouth. *Life's furrows make men more attractive. White streaks in his curly black hair. Fox wins the aging battle.*

Was there a battle?

Grace twirls her stool back to the mirror to break the spell. To gain control. *There's always a battle, somehow.*

Fox strolls behind her and runs his hands across her shoulders and neck. The shiver returns.

"Are you cold, sweetheart? Or is it me."

It isn't a question. Her husband rubs her shoulders and kisses her cheek. His hands drop down the front of her T-shirt.

"I think it is me, pet," he whispers in her ear. He kisses her neck gently, then more. His passion shimmers as he works to control himself.

Fox straddles Grace on the stool, balancing his weight on his muscular legs, taking her head in his big hands to kiss her. He singsongs in his low murmur, like a lullaby, driving a storm through her. A siren call.

His vocal foreplay. Warning me.

"I was lost in you from the first day. I saw you, and my breathing stopped. If I couldn't sing—" he whispers, "—would I have ever had a chance?"

Drumming pounds in her ears, and the fire roars. Grace lifts her head and closes her eyes, falling into him. She runs her hands through his unruly hair. *Why do I struggle?*

I just want choices. In everything.

Suddenly, Grace falls into a vacuum. Her body stops working, and the desire drops from her like a blanket to the ground. I

Into the blackness. Gone. She squeezes her eyes shut.

Oh, God.

Fox hesitates, raising his eyes to hers. "Am I plodding?" He cocks his head like he often does, his eyes fighting a flash of hurt. His voice brittle. Reactions are so small that only Grace can catch them.

He's so vulnerable. Faced with her husband's distress, she mellows. "No, no, honey. I'm having trouble. Hot flashes."

Climbing off his wife's lap, Fox kneels on the floor. "Apparently, the only flash was me, flashing by myself."

As he fights his disappointment, Grace glimpses the rage inside. *Anger at his failure to manage his emotions.*

"Not true." She drops to the floor beside him. "My estrogen is bailing on me. I'm walking about with sandpaper shoved up my hoo-ha. We were together, and a switch threw." She stumbles through her words, knowing her husband and his demons.

Scrambling.

Once again, the lost, awkward girl, trapped in a traitorous, drooping, stranger's body.

An old woman's body. Failing me. "I have a present for you, sweet Lad. For us."

Fox's mouth is a tight line, but Grace stands and skips into the bathroom before he can object. Back in an instant, she climbs onto his lap.

"Here, give me your hand." She turns her husband's palm upward, squirting a silky fluid from a pink bottle. The lotion smells like a honey biscuit, which Grace thought was apt when she bought it, refusing to look into the cashier's seventeen-year-old eyes.

"You are the best-looking almost fifty-year-old ever," she whispers, rubbing his chest. "Sexy, soft, white curls."

"They aren't all white," Fox chuckles, the tension gone.

"No. Some are gray." She kisses him, leading them into what he calls 'our private garden.' Closing the world out. Grace understands too well. She went in the first time, and part of her never returned.

"What is this stuff?" Fox mumbles. "It tingles. Oh, my." He kisses Grace's face, her nose, her mouth. "I love you. I love you. I love you. Always, forever."

Her husband's obsessive focus is a gift in their private life. She's his, and he's dedicated to pleasing her, always putting her needs first. "It's a dance, darling girl," he repeats. I hear your music, I play your sonnet, and we dance—soft, and sweet, and slow."

"My unselfish maestro," she whispers into his neck, kissing right below his ear. "My favorite spot."

He groans, shuddering. "How can I be so lost in you for so long?"

―――

Lying on the carpet in the darkness, her husband turns his head away. His reaction to their lovemaking confused her for a while at their beginning, then she saw the tears one day. Sometimes, an urge to comfort him rises, but she'll never give in.

"A magic elixir," Fox sighs.

Grace laughs. "It is a magic elixir, my generous and dangerous Ladislaw. Pharma magic for aging lovers."

"I don't know any aging lovers. If I find any, I'm going to recommend this potion to them. I'm keeping this in my nightstand." Fox kisses the top of his wife's head and examines the bottle. "I will say this, though. An aging lover would have a desperate need to get off this floor before becoming paralyzed."

He hops up, leaning to pluck Grace from the floor. "Come, my pet, my darling girl. Let's test our new weapon again." He sweeps her to the king-sized bed dominating the bedroom.

"Yeah, *wight*," she laughs, a joke from the past.

Marley's past.

―――

The couple lies together, silent, retreating from oneness into separation. At this point, Grace has an urge to run. Run to a secluded place of her own.

Her husband struggles with physical touch, even from her, if it comes without warning. He explains the feeling is 'like I've been burned or shocked.' Yet, in sleep, Fox is what she secretly calls a clamorer. He clings and wriggles into her space until he relaxes.

Keeping me awake.

Well, something keeps me awake. My husband or my menopause.

"When you fake, I feel it," he says, snuggling into her side. Grace reels on him. "I never fake." Tinged with guilt, caught and confronted. *This is like you,* she rails in silence. *Defend your secret suffering and demand everyone else surrender their souls.*

She grits her teeth. *His dictates are like tiny thieves, stealing my essence heartbeat at a time.*

He's blissfully unaware.

"Yes, you do." Fox's voice holds its utter gentleness.

Always gentle, like I'm fragile. I'm a flower, and you're the wind and rain whipping against me.

His lips brush against her shoulder as he speaks. "Pet, what's real is all that's important." He gazes at her, all sweetness. "A betrayal of a kind."

"Fox." She grinds out the name.

"It's no good. Promise me, I mean it. Faking is done for." Steel fills his placid green eyes through those thick black lashes. "I need to know."

"Of course, husband."

If he hears her sarcasm, he ignores it, murmuring 'Yes' and kissing her cheek.

There's no faking anything tonight. Heat rises in her chest. *Why does he tread on the precious things?* She rolls her back to him.

How are we so one and not one at the same time?

Grace won't sleep tonight. She'll blame menopause this time.

two
early morning—the second day

"LISTEN, FOX." Captain Skip Harley stands behind his immaculate desk in his pristine, glassed-in office, straightening neatly stacked papers. Cap's office sits like a rhinestone in the grungy detective's area of Violent Crimes in the Palm Beach County Sheriff's Office. "I'm worried about these assaults, too. I care about the victims, too."

"Hmm."

The senior officer looks up at his subordinate. "Politics is a real thing here, and if the fact slips past you, Dr. Argall, well, too fucking bad."

Fox shuffles, dark eyebrows drawn together. His square jaw flexes as he works to stay patient, shoving his fists into his pockets.

"This whole thing—" Cap grasps for his point. He's more irritated than he should be. "This thing is complicated. I'm worried, well, about a lot of things." Turning away, he disentangles from his lieutenant to fixate on his array of orchids lined up halfway down the office wall and located, of course, for the exact light. A tiny bug crawls up one of his splendid blooms. The captain picks the insect off, rolling the bug between his thumb and forefinger.

Fox Argall always stares at me like I'm this bug—like he pities me somehow. He could squash me any second, but he doesn't want to, so he consents to let me live.

Cap hesitates a beat longer to hold the appearance of dominance, waiting to glance up. "Well?"

"It's a case." Fox exhales and does his empty blink-thing. "We'll work like every case. No different. Tick and I give each one the same effort. Everything we've got."

The patented Argall intensity. He stands there like he's calm, but I can hear the volcano inside. Damn, how does the guy not drop dead from the exhaustion of being Fox fucking Argall? A scab itching my work-fifteen-hours-a-day life.

A blaze shoots through Cap, but he forces a laugh. "Look, genius boy. Your fevered insistence on ignoring my reality, the politics of this damned station, changes nothing." He will never let Fox Argall see him sweat. He tweaks him as a habit to remind him.

To remind me.

The detective's brows flit down, always avoiding contact. Fox fights to maintain a neutral expression, but Cap reads the frustration roiling in the brain behind those weird eyes. His lieutenant is frozen in an awkward stance, like a deer ready to run.

Realization hits the senior officer. *Fuck. He has no idea why I'm bitching.*

The hallmark blank expression, a sign of Fox's daily struggle, deflates him. "Yeah, OK, this is nothing new—a case. Where the hell are you now, Dr. Argall? You and your boy Tick? Where is your partner? Not here."

The detective draws his eyebrows down again, twisting his mouth.

Taking the bait on Tick, as always. "Reaching into your encyclopedia brain under 'human behavior' to find why your boss is so pissed?"

Fox squares his jaw again, raising his chin. Dragging his eyes up. Blank eyes. Connecting for a mere moment before he cocks his head and disengages.

Cap swallows a smile as his lieutenant glances at him, the slight interaction enough to show a defiant flash sparking. *Welcome back, laddie. Don't stay up on the porch like a plonker. Come run with the big boys.* "Summarize."

"We have DNA. Mitochondrial DNA from a hair." Evolving into the professor, Fox enunciates carefully, in low tones, drifting to the wall-length window. He slows to examine the orchids over his boss's shoulder, crowding him, brushing Cap's jacket before continuing. "An intact bulb at the end of the strand, but we haven't established age, so a profile may or may not be obtainable. The hair is red, rather bright, and thick. Works in our favor. Easier to confirm."

Cap forces himself to water an orchid as his lieutenant veers into his personal space. "So, you've got minor useful stuff to tell us some minor useful thing," he says, but he understands the science as well as the scientist-turned-criminologist. One last poke. The skirmish is over. No one cares who won.

"DNA gives us the picture, but we need to find a suspect." Fox leans against the window sill, crosses his legs in front of him, and narrows his eyes at his captain. Rancor is now carefully hidden. There's no mention of Tick. The mask is back up.

"Let's find one."

Worry flickers so quickly across his detective's face that Cap almost misses it. He doesn't miss much. "What?"

"Nothing. Some additional paths we're running down."

He's working to keep his face straight. Cap focuses on the detective, examining his expression before waving him away. "Go, get after your case."

Half an hour later, Detective Sergeant John Tickman saunters in. He throws his empty holster on his desk.

Fox sits on his adjoining desktop, on his phone.

Waiting.

Eyeing his partner, Tick says, "You're here early."

"Repeating this phrase every morning will not make it so, nor will your words wash away your incessant tardiness." The older man walks off, motioning toward the hallway.

Tick messes with a few papers on his desk to waste time and follows Fox to the coffee room.

Tick accepts the steaming coffee his partner offers him. "What's up, man? You look like a dog that got beat."

"Nah, had a long night." Fox shuffles his feet and brushes at a nonexistent piece of lint on his spotless trousers.

This means his boss isn't going to tell him squat. *Flipping me his charming smile, but his downcast eyes say something else.* He files the exchange away. "You meet with Cap yet?"

"Yeah, like every morning, *consigliere*." Fox cocks his head, rolling his eyes as he pulls his phone from his pocket. "He wants us hard on the assault cases. I told him we were, had DNA, but no match." His Welsh accent deepens. "He was a bit agitated, y'know." The accent always grows stronger in disquiet.

"Yes, I know." Tick sets his coffee cup on the counter. "This is literally the worst coffee on the planet, to go with the worst case of my career."

"A nightmare," Fox agrees, frowning. "Our two boys. Thrown into the brush at two ends of the county? Dunno. On first pass, any connection appears unlikely. But they feel related."

"All this political bullshit on the news." Tick grimaces. "Damn, the media's going nuts. Assholes looking to make more shit are slipping in like snakes from every direction. We're lucky they haven't heard who caught the case. I wanna keep everything quiet despite my infamous partner."

"Warning received."

"I got no truck with media or any politicians, especially the ones who only run into a place when real people face genuine pain." *Like vampires, swooping to set their teeth in desperate folks who are twitching for a fix. Their fifteen minutes. Sick.* "Vampires." Tick doesn't realize he's speaking aloud.

"What are you thinking, pet? Now who's merked?"

"Don't call me 'pet.'" Tick growls. "Thinking about those scumbag rabble-rousing assholes yammering about this case and how I want to be invisible until we put this mess to bed. Fucking vampires. Now your shit's all over me, damn."

"Glad for it to do a bunk." Fox tilts his head, offering rare eye contact. He waves his hand to the exit. "We're off. Need to meet with forensics."

"Bunk you, you English jerk," the younger man grouses, leading his partner out. "You been here thirty freaking years. Why don't you talk English?"

"I am *not* English. I'm Welsh. And I think you mean, 'Why don't you speak an American dialect?' I speak English quite well. We spoke the language long before you Yanks."

Tick sticks his arm behind his back and flips his middle finger.

The older man meanders behind his sergeant, twisting his cell phone in his pocket, a constant rustling.

"You're like walking with a toddler. If I didn't lead you to the parking lot, you'd wander off and get lost," Tick snarks. "Full-time job to keep my eye on you, Dr. Argall. Like you notice."

"Hmm."

Fox never notices. He's just waiting for enough time to pass before he can begin a new game of Brick Breaker.

Grace says her husband's playing in the company of others is rude, but Tick recognizes the self-stimulation. *Hiding. Distraction.* His partner reminds him of his baby brother, Jackson. He understands the signs. He had to know them. Jackson was his to protect.

Tick was the kid born with grown-up responsibility, and he can't remember a time when he didn't fight for calm. Anxiety shadowed every moment, threatening to swamp him.

The sergeant got his younger brother Jackson out of high school from a bad part of Riviera Beach and off to college. He finally felt like he'd earned the right to breathe. For so long, only Jack mattered. His brother went to Florida State on a scholarship in aeronautical engineering. NASA hired Jack straight out of college.

Jack settled at NASA, and Tick let his guard down, falling like so many other kids. He went on a year-long bender. When Jack announced NASA had chosen him for a chance to be the first black astronaut on the moon, he knew it was time to stop spinning. Tick went after and won a scholarship to study English Literature, which earned him more harassment than he could ever explain. He always loved Yeats.

Tick earned his degree with honors. On the way home from the graduation ceremony, he saw a recruiting office and walked in. He spent the next decade jumping out of planes into various places, none of which were rational. For no particular reason at no particular time, his military stint had served its purpose. He came home and went right into the Police Academy.

The south Florida humidity sweeps over them as the automatic doors slide open, dragging Tick back to the present. "Gonna be a hot one today," he says, putting on his sunglasses.

Fox's cell blares. Cap's ring. Tick's phone sets off a second later. Cap's admin, Missy.

"Shit. This can't be good," Tick groans.

Fox twirls his fingers, mouthing, "Here we go." He stabs the 'answer' icon with a finger. "Argall," he says, moving away.

"Yup," Tick says into his phone. "We're still in the parking lot, Missy. Tell Cap we're headed back." Spinning theatrically on his heel, he dances back to the doors, drawing a head tilt from his partner.

The men turn out of the bright Florida sunlight and disappear into the cool, mirrored Sheriff's building.

This is gonna be a long day.

three
morning—the second day

"WE FOUND ANOTHER YOUNG VICTIM." Cap's voice is tight. "The scene is in Abacoa by the stadium."

Fox jerks.

Damn. Tick groans. *This close to his Gracie? Damn.*

"Yes, close to your house, Lieutenant." Cap nods. "A bad one, boys, so be prepared as you make the scene. Off Military Trail, the wetland between Dakota and Indian Creek. Almost across from the Hungarian bakery."

The captain punches his index finger at the detectives. "Don't even glance at any reporters. Dammit. Get going, and don't let any 'commenting' come back to me. Put your heads down and walk past every fucking one. Got me? Call me as soon as you have a handle on everything."

As the partners leave Cap's office, he slaps his hands on his desk and yells. "Check in! What the hell am I going to tell these mayors who are on my ass? Damn, next, the governor will be calling. Fuck."

―――

Tick merges onto A1A and grumbles, "Traffic is worse every year. This crime scene is smack dab in the Abacoa development, yards from Military Trail. It's a far cry from the Loxahatchee Refuge."

"Smack dab," Fox repeats, locked on his game. "Escalating risk."

Abacoa is a brick-street, tree-filled, planned community. Fox and Grace live near the Florida Atlantic University Honors Campus, across from Roger Dean Stadium. The stadium is Abacoa's centerpiece, drawing tourists every baseball season.

When the developers designed the area, they left sections untouched to offset the builds. The wetland separates Abacoa from Military Trail. They fenced the brush with wooden pathways winding through a natural environment accommodating wildlife with nowhere else to go.

Wild pigs, gators, snakes... What else is in here? Tick shudders. "I hate snakes. And bugs."

Fox doesn't answer.

"I love baseball, so there's a plus," Tick continues. "Anything laid out like a scene from Stepford Wives would generally annoy the hell out of me, but I really like Abacoa." The saving grace is the Roger Dean baseball stadium. He spends his free time in the Argalls' backyard and the sports field. Both feel like home. "Any ideas about the location, Fox? Why so close to so many people? Why is he escalating, if he is?"

"Brick Breaker, gimme a second."

"Don't let my witless banter interrupt your concentration." Tick understands the constant game-playing. Anyone needs a vent in this job. His partner needs more than most. The problem for Tick is the silence while he plays.

Fox exhales, putting his phone on his lap. "Yes, right in the middle of Abacoa. Full, busy neighborhoods—my neighborhood, in fact. Close to Military Trail and feet from a major throughway." His long fingers flip his device from front to back, over and over.

Itching to begin another game. "We're going in through Abacoa's side streets, not off Military. Off Linsmore. Try to miss the throng," Tick says. His partner doesn't care.

He won't even notice.

Play parks with swing sets and slides dot the development, which has several schools, from kindergarten through senior high.

"This is next to a junior high and an elementary." Tick sighs.

"Yes." Fox grinds his jaw, frowning. He flips his thumbs across the phone screen. "Spring break. Think there'll be kids?"

"There are always kids, all the time." Tick grips the steering wheel. "A traffic cluster is building ahead. A satellite truck from WPEC. WFLX, already here before us."

Fox flicks his eyes at his partner, then returns to his game.

Spring training is underway, and the baseball fields are full. The area enjoys massive tourism during the spring, especially if the St. Louis Cardinals—who win pennants and World Series—are doing well. Tick's been waiting for the Miami Marlins to win since elementary school.

Is this bastard local or riding in with the fans? Tick swings left at Frederick Small. "A local?"

"Dunno. Or a tourist."

"Well, thanks for shit. Never thought of that." Tick's shoulders tighten. He rolls through a relaxation technique he learned in the military. One muscle at a time, unwind down your body. "Your genius for the obvious."

Fox shrugs at the younger man. "Insufficient data."

"Your damn game, Shay."

"Shay," Fox mumbles. "Will it ever grow old?"

"Nah." The first time Tick called Fox 'Seamus,' his colleague had a hysterical fit. Went on forever about where Ireland was, how Ireland wasn't Wales and why were Americans ignorant dogs? *Cha. Ching.* "Not as long as it makes me laugh."

The detective gives his partner a quick side-eye. "Last level, mate. Give me a second."

Tick grumbles, "Well, s'cuse me, mardy," in a bad English accent and grins at his cleverness. He pulls into the quiet cul-de-sac on Linsmore Lane and can't find a safe place to park. *If someone spots us, we seriously look like cops.*

They return to Dakota Road and hoof to the woods off Linsmore. The humidity thickens as they enter the shadowed glade, and sweat soaks Tick's shirt. A pungent, earthy smell of decaying vegetation hits them in a wave.

"I hate this muck," Tick grouses. Twisted roots heap in piles on the path, and murky water sloshes in his shoes with each sinking step. A bird screeches through the dense foliage. The sergeant jumps. "Damn, this place is creepy."

Fox glances at him, narrowing his eyes, but doesn't speak.

Sweat beads on Tick's neck, stinging and attracting bugs. "I hate these damn bugs." He swipes at himself frantically, earning a glare and frown from his partner.

As they come through the woods, lights sparkle in the thick brush ahead: overhead spotlights.

Forensic lights.
Dammit, everyone's arrived before us.

A buzzing cluster of white safety suits gather at a tree about fifty yards into the brush. A uniformed deputy is stationed about halfway to the group, blocking access. Fox wanders to her, his head still in his game. "Stace," he purrs, giving the young woman a charming smile. She turns furiously red.

Does he understand his effect on people?

"Dr. Argall." Deputy Stacey Gonzales faces the older man. "Team arrived. Medical examiner close; be here inside 15 minutes."

Fox's eyes cloud at the information. "Medical examiner?" He glances at the group standing around the boy and sighs vacantly at Stacey, who nods, her face dark.

"Yes. Dr. Gaffley is *en route*."

"Thanks, Stace. Block Linsmore Lane off, would you? No one goes through but has a house. Not a copper block, no tape. Just horses. Use the city's. No one through, yes? Good girl, you."

His dark brow furrows, and he mutters something Stacey and Tick don't need to hear to understand. He shakes like a dog flipping off water and starts to the turmoil, his fists shoved deep in his pockets.

"Shay," Tick calls. "You need gloves and booties, Scientist Man." He pulls plastic packages from the box next to Stacey and tosses one to his partner.

"Hate these things," Fox moans as he repeatedly adjusts his fingers. "Not gonna touch anything."

"You spent how many years as a researcher and physician? How did hating gloves work?"

"Had my own."

"Of course you did. A consideration to solve the present challenge."

Fox cocks his head and rolls his eyes. "Not planning to touch anything," he repeats.

The partners trudge to a cluster of law enforcement personnel. As they arrive, Chief Medical Examiner Ezequiel Gaffley crosses through the deep brush from Military Trail to join them.

"Wassup?" Ez throws the question out as he circles the slight form slumped against the crooked tree, pulling on his gloves.

Ez's dad was American, his mother is Cuban. He's calm, smart, and will take your feet out if you cross him. The medical examiner might reasonably be on the Annoyed By Fox Team, considering the detective holds advanced degrees he rarely uses. Fox's academic credentials annoy people, especially other highly educated ones. Ez doesn't care. He wouldn't want to lose his seat at the Argall table for football games.

"Grace is quite the cook," the medical examiner explained one day. "The key to your best life is knowing your priorities."

"You tell us what's up, Doc." Tick waves his hand dissolutely at a young boy tied against the tree, clearly dead.

The child's head lies to the side, cheek down on the scrub pine's rough bark. His eyes are closed, his dark, damp hair clinging to his forehead.

Appears peaceful. Asleep. The bile rushes into Tick's throat as he struggles to stay where he's standing. All he wants to do is run.

Ez strolls the scene, occasionally squatting to peer at the

victim. "Gimme time. He's about twelve, thirteen, no older. Might be Caucasian, maybe not. Small frame."

"Cause of death later?" Tick warns Ez to silence. *I don't want the information out in this crowd.* Ez glances at the sergeant and then at Fox. "'Course, can't say. Gotta take him in. No news for a while. Full schedule. Can't hurry, yes?"

Ez hates politics. Probably jonesing for a cigar. I don't smoke, and I want a cigar.

"Push these guys back, yes?" Ez motions to his aides to bring his kit and waves at the group surrounding the body. "Need room."

"Move, everyone. Give the doc the space he needs." The sergeant waves his fingers to the crew to widen the circle. "Set a perimeter. No one comes in here, understand? Jan and Tazo, you're in charge of protecting this area. I want someone on this scene until I say so. Do not screw me. I take that personal." *This is my place. In the lead. If not me, who?*

"Tick." His partner is standing behind him, holding out his glove, which is no longer on his hand. "Look."

Fox unfolds the blue glove to show Tick a jeweled, scruffy pin. *A ladies' pin. An odd old lady pin.* "A pin?" The area is dense with shrubs and near the streets. "Shay, man. Houses are a stone's throw. Someone could easily drop something like this."

"I dunno. Familiar somehow." The detective tilts his head and studies the pin. "I'm bagging it."

"Bag it, man." Tick shrugs.

A uniform stands in the distance with a woman Tick doesn't recognize. He elbows his partner. "Who's Dennis talking to?"

"Don't know. I'll run her off." Fox starts toward them before Tick grabs him.

"No, shit, man. She's media, and you're made. We don't want Cap pissed, and I don't want those assholes knowing it's our case."

The Ruin of the Watcher

Fox is well-known to the local media. His notoriety drags Tick into any swamp he wanders into. Literally and figuratively.

Tick motions to the nearest deputy. "Check if the lady with Dennis is news and shove her off."

"These stones might be real." His partner is staring at the pin.

"Think this guy is a burglar?" Tick shrugs again. "The perp's DNA isn't in the system, but if he hasn't been caught? Seriously, man, what's in that brain of yours? We're feet away from, like, masses of people."

"Who comes in this wetland off the planking? Wild pigs are enough to keep anyone out." Fox shakes his head, rubbing his neck. "Taking this pin for sign-off. What do you think about race? Seems white to me."

"Seems white to me, too." He grimaces at the small, frail body. "Changes the politics."

"Yes, the politics." Fox twitches. "I'm signing this pin in."

four
late morning—the second day

"GRACE? Gracie, can you hear me? I'm walking back to the car. We've got another." Fox sounds distant.

"Another—? I'm so sorry, honey. Are they bringing him here? Another boy?" Grace sits in her bioethics office at Jupiter Inlet Hospital, reviewing the file for the previous assault, a boy named Deacon Matthews. Deacon is on the fifth floor. The child is tiny, frail, and unconscious. *Filled with tubes. Surrounded by cops and fussing relatives.*

"No need, love, no one gets this little one anymore. Tick and I are coming to the hospital. We have to mix on this."

"Ah, honey. I'm so sorry." Grace blinks away a flash of tears. "What time? Meet me in my office?" *He sounds so tired.*

She doesn't understand why her husband decided to be a cop. He worked hard in medical school to be a researcher and physician. Started over again at law school. She understood when he gave up the law. He was unhappy in Boston with the job and the firm. *Giving up medicine? I will never understand that one.*

The familiar pressure builds in her chest.

Don't come here. I don't want to know.

Her husband's voice drags her back. "Now OK? Can you meet us in the boy's room?"

"Of course, yes. His room might not be the best place to talk."

Grace hesitates. "Stel's hands are full—like she's managing a skirmish at the U.N."

"Who's bad? Family? Outsiders? Who else?"

"Family's fine. Outsiders, media, everyone else is bad. About once a day, someone tries to set a press conference in the kid's room. Damned people sneak around. Stel's at the end of her rope. No work done for babysitting the *hoi polloi*. In the truest Greek, of course."

"Of course. How else?" Fox chuckles. "Ten minutes 'til we arrive. Can you ask Stel to help you clear 'em off the floor? Tick wants to stay *incognito*."

The spouses say 'Latin' at the same time, making Grace giggle.

"My girl," Fox murmurs in his soft lilt, and heat shoots through her.

We're a chemical reaction.

Ten minutes later, Fox and Tick pull into the emergency room parking lot. They enter through the ER, which is infamous. It is always full, day and night. People are distracted, in pain, and frustrated. A constant low buzz, broken with periodic bursts of moaning and occasional anger fills the space. Patients sit in wheelchairs and stand against walls with their families. On bad days, stretchers line the hallway past the entry door.

Few people pay attention to anyone coming in the emergency entrance unless they're looking to complain. Noses in their navels, deep in their own fear or frustration. It's easy for the detectives to slip in unnoticed.

The staff recognizes the partners. Today, the lovely dark-haired nurse smiles at them and buzzes them through a back way, minimizing any attention. Tick blushes and glances at Fox.

The detective is gritting his teeth, his jaw muscles flexed. Tick can't hold in a snort. *Holding his breath, walking through the ER. Hilarious.*

Tick walks backward to face the older man. "You called Grace? How come?" He shrugs. "I don't care, but a little off for you. Usually, we show with no warning. Not the pattern to announce yourself."

Startled out of his breath-holding concentration, Fox inhales and purses his lips. Tick grins as his partner recovers his all-important poise.

"I think we have some delicate issues here, and I want to make sure we have everything covered," Fox says, irritated at the interruption of his routine. "Why are you rambling in reverse?"

"Ethically? Or politically? What are you thinking? What will Grace do?"

Grace Argall practices at several hospitals in the area. *I don't know much about her. Or my partner, come to think. Except he went to a bunch of schools.*

Fox frowns. "I'm not sure."

"Delicate for the family, the other assault?" Tick presses. "We're not sure about a connection. This one is probably white and certainly dead." He stops in the hallway. "Spill, man. What's your plan? You've decided something."

"The pin." Fox hesitates, eyes flicking down. "This last one is connected. Same guy. There was a lot of assuming after the first two were black. This is a matter of convenience, not race. Well, not race, but build. All slender, young-looking. Could be the same boy, if not for varying shades. And not a tourist. This is a local or someone who knows the area well."

"You decide this from a fancy pin?" Tick dances in an urge to lighten the surrounding air. "Damnation, Shay, I got me the best frickin' partner on the planet. The universe!"

"Ridiculous," Fox mutters.

"Sherlock Freaking Holmes." He grins at his partner. "Shit. Is that bloke Irish? I sure don't want to hurt your sweet Welsh feelings."

Fox tips his head to the side, as he often does, and bares his straight, white teeth.

Like my Jack Russell Terrier. My Rottie would be a better comparison to Fox. Gentle until the bark, then he's coming at you.

"Well, maybe not only the pin." Fox sits on a chair in the hallway. "The assaults are exactly the same. Anal penetration. No prophylactic. Minor bruising on the arms where he holds them. Scrapes on the wrists from the rope. The rope is rough, about a quarter of an inch wide. Scratches and bruising on the forehead and cheek where he pushes them against a tree. This one will have drugs on board, too. Same ones. Mix of Demerol and midazolam."

"Man," Tick whispers. "I hate this shit."

Fox's voice lowers to a murmur. "In some ways, the drugs are unusual in their mercy. With those drugs, the boys can't form short-term memories. They won't remember everything happening to them. They may never remember."

"This one is dead." Tick reminds him. "What's cause of death?"

"Incidental to the attack. I think Ez will find this one aspirated and choked."

He's worked something out. Tick is sure his partner is correct. *He keeps everything locked inside his head until he's certain.* "OK, so we meet Grace. What for?"

"We need permission from the family for a procedure."

"A procedure," Tick says. "I'm not going to argue. I don't have forty-seven damn degrees. Whatever you say, goes. How do we do this?"

"Technically, two procedures." Fox draws out his thoughts. "We need the families of both boys, all three if we can. I want them to agree. The kids to assent themselves. The ones alive."

Like that part would confuse me.

"And I want a blood test. Grace will manage her end." Fox starts walking again, his jaw tight. "I'm not sure she'll be happy with me."

Why does the bioethicist need to manage it? "Well, man, she's your wife. If you can't handle her, no one can."

Fox scoffs. "I'm not the man, nor have I met the man who 'handles' Grace."

"Don't look at me, Shay," Tick snickers. "Grace scares me more than you do. I'll take on Stel before I'd go at Grace."

A cool breeze swooshes from the elevator doors, and three people step out with lanyards and recording equipment.

Media.

The partners duck their heads and enter the lift. The doors slide shut, and the elevator voice announces: *'Fifth floor.'*

five
noon—the second day

THE ELEVATOR DOORS SLIDE OPEN, and Grace greets them as they step out onto the fifth floor.

This will be rough. Tick glances at his partner's placid expression. *He's putting on the calm.*

Fox glides to his wife and brushes a red curl from her forehead. "Morning, love. Not an agreeable morning, though."

"Wouldn't appear so. I'm sorry, honey." Grace touches her husband's hand, searching his expression before turning to Tick. "Sorry, so sorry. Never gets easier."

The big man shrugs, frowning. *Never.* "Harder for the family."

Grace's cheeks flush, and tears spring to her blue eyes. "I see it more often than most and can't begin to imagine."

"Uh-hmm." Stella Parks stands at the nurse's station, glaring at the men. The head nurse cleared the hallways, leaving only the uniforms stationed by the patient's door. Pointing at the partners, she says, "Gentlemen. Note the situation on this floor—my floor —can change without notice."

Sounds like my sixth-grade teacher.

"May we go in?" Fox nods toward the glass partition separating the room from the hall.

The detective opens the door and flicks his fingers to motion

Grace and Tick inside without waiting for Stel. A tiny, still figure lies in the hospital bed, almost hidden by the machinery surrounding him. Light streams across his passive face from a half-wall of windows atop a vented, beige heating unit, spewing metallic racket into the room.

This place is freezing. Hospitals are always so cold. Bitter odors on my tongue.

Wires cross the boy's shallow chest, endotracheal tubing stretching the small mouth open. Multiple IV drip trees surround him, forming a metal forest. The ventilator's swoosh, swoosh, swoosh punctuates the icy, medical cacophony.

This little guy. What kind of twist does this shit? How does this evil look in the light?

The head nurse stomps in beside them, focused on Fox.

Fox is ignoring Stel. Heat flares in Tick's chest. *It's aggressive. He's thrown a barrier between them. Why? What is he doing?*

A pink flush colors Grace's neck. Panic flashes across her face before she collects herself.

She sees what he's doing. What's with him?

"He's still on propofol," Stel warns. "He can't talk."

"Yes, yes. No matter. Chart, please." Fox strides deep into the brightly lit hospital room.

Stella throws her hip out, elbow akimbo. She stares at the detective's back, eyes blazing. "You got release?"

The air chills as she challenges him.

Fox flinches.

Damnation. Did I imagine his reaction? His partner's face rights itself into compassion. *A mask.* "We got the release. In the chart, correct?" Tick lays his hand on Stel's shoulder.

The nurse jerks loose from Tick and storms out the door, her sturdy clogs thumping the ward floor's no-color linoleum.

Fox doesn't react to the drama. He roams to the young boy's bed, checking meds. He raises the sheet to examine the child's feet and legs, pausing at his right knee.

"Ticker, a deep contusion on his knee, not where we'd expect. Can you note it?"

The physician-turned-criminologist leans in and assesses the smooth forehead with its black spiral curls, moving to inspect the stick-thin arms. He avoids touching the child. Finally, he examines the boy's hands, which are too large for the small body.

Acid fills Tick's throat. *He's a puppy, sweet and floppy.*

Stella slips in behind them, wheeling an electronic medical record cart. She places a foot on the bottom and shoves the stand at the detective.

The room goes still. Fox freezes, his mouth tightening. A second later, he walks to Stella and cups his hands on her cheeks. Their initial words fade under the vent's irritating swoosh and the automatic dispenser swishing drugs into the young boy on the bed.

The nurse's voice rises. "Ellis, he's completely vulnerable."

"Stel, pet, do you believe I want to harm this boy? You've determined I'm his enemy?" Fox's lyrical voice is soft, but his pale gaze is stony. He sighs, whispering, "I'm aware he's yours to protect."

Stella squeezes her eyes shut as he continues. "No one in this room wants this darling boy to hurt anymore. Let's keep the menace straight." Their foreheads are almost touching. His words are a demand.

A tear rolls down the woman's face. Fox brushes her cheek with his thumb and hugs her tight. The two stand together for a minute. Stel touches Fox's jaw and approaches the bed.

Tick works to keep his mouth closed. *He's hugging her? What does Grace think about this stuff? I'd never get away with it. People don't recognize they're being managed.*

Or they ignore it.

Stel gestures to the child. "Here. I showed his physicians. You need to see, too." She lifts the boy's arm, revealing a metallic patch inside a circle drawn from a medical marker. A tiny dot shines in his hairless underarm. "This peculiar little sparkle thing embedded here."

Fox peers at the pin-size spot. "Wasn't he x-rayed?"

"Well, maybe not in his armpit."

"Yes, well." He repeats. Blinking, he shuffles and presses his lips tight. "Let's sort the order, shall we?"

"Yes, Dr. Argall."

Fox flashes his eyebrows and smiles vaguely. "Thanks, Mrs. Parks."

Tick realizes he's been holding his breath. He exhales as Grace takes her husband's arm to usher him out.

"Use your powers wisely, Lad," she whispers.

"What kinda voodoo shit, Stel?" Tick murmurs into the nurse's ear.

Stel shifts like a snake striking and pinches him hard in the soft spot on his side. Tick shrieks.

"Quiet, this is a hospital," she hisses.

Out in the hall, Fox twirls his funny dance, his tell when he's trapped. "Gracie, we—we, we've got an issue. It's not a muck-up, not really. No one would have been in a place to understand at first. Anyway, there it is." He throws his hands in the air, stammering as he searches for the ideal way to approach his point.

Grace stands noiselessly, watching him.

Fox flips from careless control in the hospital room to uneasy shuffling in the face of his unsympathetic wife. Grace lets her husband fidget.

She's not going to help him. Aching to break the tension, Tick steps toward the couple. Stel squeezes his arm to stop him.

"Obviously, Gracie, a violent pedophile is in the area." Fox waves his hand at the boy's room. He shifts his weight from foot to foot in his awkward shimmy. "I'm guessing the perp is infected. Possibly with more than one disease."

He's desperate, begging.

"STDs we can track. We can develop the pathogens' molecular typing using pulsed-field gel electrophoresis at the forensic lab. Pray luck will find us." Fox pushes his fists deep into his pocket, flipping his phone. The rustling material screeches in the tense silence.

"What? A blood pull?" Grace laughs in relief. "I thought you were working to ask me to cut the child's hand off the way you wriggled. I didn't want to know."

The atmosphere thickens as Fox stands silent.

Oh, shit, man. This is a bad one. Tick retreats a few steps from the couple.

"OK. I laughed too soon." Grace stares up at her husband, who is a foot taller than the tiny woman. "Say what you're thinking. Out with what you want."

Fox leans down, almost nose to nose, engaging his wife in a force field. "We need a colonoscopy."

Tick gasps out loud as Stella exhales and whirls, stamping her feet down the hall.

"A colonoscopy." Grace shivers.

Fox grimaces and nods. "Yes."

"On an eleven-year-old boy who has been violently assaulted." Her voice is low and robotic.

"If he wakes, consent is required." Fox's gaze and tone remain steady and gentle as he forges through. "We'll need assent, too."

"My job, Ellis," Grace says quietly.

Damn. 'Ellis.' This can't be good.

A commotion starts in the hallway, at the corner by the elevator. Voices argue and grow louder.

Stel stops mid-way to the nurse's station as the four turn to the noise. "You boys. Leave. Down the stairs at the other end. Grace will meet you in her office. Git." The nurse wheels on her chunky heels and heads into the chaos.

The men take off down the hall to the exit.

Inside the stairwell, Tick says, "Man. Why talk in the boy's room, where you shove shit down everyone's throat? Freaking. Un. Comfortable."

"Because I needed to examine the boy first, and everyone

needs to realize I'm right. To help them handle the situation." Fox takes the stairs two at a time. "And you find out the best things when you make people uncomfortable."

Tick sighs and follows his partner up the stairs. Some load has lifted from his shoulders. *What happened?*

⸺

Grace's office is good-sized and almost unfurnished. Somehow, she manages to leave the room cramped. Magazines are stacked in piles, some still in their plastic covers. Books lay scattered on the single bookcase. Highlighted papers scrawled with red markings bound by giant clips are spread on the floor surrounding the empty desk. A random chair is near the door, not facing anything.

Tick hesitates at the door. *Grace is so elegant. Her home is spotless. What's this mess about?*

Fox sits on his wife's desk and stretches his long legs, opening Brick Breaker on his phone. They both turn when the door opens.

A man in a flat-out superb suit strolls in. Lilac stripes in green plaid. The material flows like water over his curated figure, accomplished with just enough show muscles to strain the shoulders.

Expensive. Damn. That is one spectacular tie.

The man leans into Fox's face. "Hello, Ellis. Where you been hiding, buddy?"

No reaction when nothing isn't right. This punk is someone.

"John Tickman, my partner." Fox sweeps his hand toward Tick without lifting his attention from the game. "Ben Fuller. Ben went to Ohio State with me. And with Grace. He's the counsel here at the hospital."

Tick nods, trying not to frown.

Fox stiffens and stares at his phone. The Brick Breaker ball bounces impotently off the screen, lost forever. He doesn't start a new game but keeps his eyes on the screen.

Did Grace call Ben to meet them here?

"Hey, John. I'm on the Ethics Committee Grace leads." Ben smiles and sticks his hand out.

"Most people call me 'Tick,'" he says, taking Ben's hand. *Fox won't put down his damn phone. I always handle the social events in this partnership.* He grins at the lawyer. "OSU, huh? Like being a Buckeye?"

"I loved being a Buckeye. We all did, right, Ellis? O - H!" Ben slaps his schoolmate's shoulder, starting the familiar cheer.

Fox remains hunched over his device. "I — O." He ends the mantra lightly enough.

No discernible stress.

Ben guffaws. The sound is forced and hollow. "Well, not as energetic as he was at the Shoe. I guess he's sober and an old fart now. We'll ask Grace whether there's energy left for anything."

Fox glances at the man without moving his head, his eyes blank.

What's between these two? Grace? Hard to imagine.

When Grace opens the door, Tick analyzes her as she takes in her husband and the hospital lawyer. *Nothing.*

"Hey, Ben, glad you're here. We need the full committee together ASAP to discuss the next steps for the young man on the fifth floor."

"What's on the docket?" Ben isn't disturbed.

Grace hasn't called him. The guy showed here on his own.

Fox relaxes his shoulders, catching the ball at the right angle on his game, knocking out the bricks.

"Blood pull and a colonoscopy with video." Grace gazes calmly at the lawyer. "Biopsy for molecular typing. Swabs to type as well." She messes with the magazines piled on her chair and doesn't sit.

"Colonoscopy? Wow." Ben's face pales. "With the damage. Quite a risk. How soon?" He grabs the random chair and sits down hard. "Why?"

"We can discuss everything at the meeting." Grace joins Tick and her husband at her desk.

Three against one. She's sending a message.

"After Fox clears the orders with the hospitalist," she continues, "we can go to the Institutional Review Board and compliance. Our committee. The families. The boys."

"After *Fox* clears the orders?" Ben spits the name. "What does *the detective* have to do with this?"

Grace and this lawyer talk about Fox like he's not five feet away, playing the fucking game.

"He requested the procedures. A blood pull and a colonoscopy." Grace isn't giving an inch in her office.

The lawyer better be prepared if he wants to thwart her. He doesn't sense the danger yet. Or doesn't care.

"Why is the *detective* ordering medical procedures?"

Can't cover anything. Or doesn't care.

"Technically, he won't order them, of course. He'll work with the hospitalist to ensure they're completed as soon as possible."

"Well." Ben coughs.

When white folks say 'well' like that, it sounds just like my Gran.

Ben glares at Fox, who still leans against Grace's desk, his expression neutral.

His thumbs aren't moving anymore.

The detective turns his head and gives the lawyer his empty-eye blink. Ben is a little pink and a lot pissed.

Pretty freakin' personal. Tick squirms.

"Well, well. Best of luck with this one—" Ben lowers his head and shrugs. "—Gracie."

Damn. 'Gracie.' A whipped dog. He's retreating for now. The stony stare says he's not gone.

Fox's shoulder twitches, shaking out a crick, but his face doesn't change.

"Luck, yes." Grace eyes the men in her office, one at a time. "Work to do, boys. Can you excuse me?"

Ben bolts for the door.

Damnation.

Fox hovers above his wife, whispering in her ear. She smiles and rubs her husband's face. He kisses her hand before he strides past Tick, and he's got the bounce back.

He won somehow.

"See ya, Grace." Tick trots after the detective, chasing him down the hall. The partners are silent until the younger man stops Fox in the ER. "Potzer pissin' in your corners?" If this Ben guy is a threat, Tick is taking Ben personally.

Fox tilts his head and half-smiles. "Potzer?"

Tick shoves him hard and stalks off.

The detective follows his colleague to the parking lot, regarding him across the car's roof.

"What, man?" Tick snarls.

"He can throw himself anywhere he wants."

Tick shakes his head. "No, damn, you don't get it. You can't let a man in your yard."

"Not my yard he wants in. Not my job to stop him." Fox drops into the passenger seat and closes the door.

"Shit, man. You do *not* understand." Tick squeezes his fists in frustration. He shakes his head again as he slams the door. "You got a woman like Grace? You got to defend the shield."

"Grace isn't my 'shield,' Tick. She chooses each moment how she acts, what she does, how she does anything. *She* chooses. I don't choose for her. I couldn't if I wanted to." He faces out the window, his jaw tight.

six
early afternoon—
the second day

CAP MOTIONS to Fox and Tick through the glass as they walk into the station. He opens his door, yelling: "Everybody! Party time. Head to chow, this floor. You two, in here." He slams the door.
Damnation. Tick flicks a glance at his partner's impassive face. *Shit.*
Everyone scurries around before moving to the break area. A detective room is like a schoolroom. Cap creates an eerily quiet environment. The enforced calm drives the sub-rosa frequency and the yammering behind the scenes. Politics exist, and sophomoric jealousy causes genuine conflict. Getting called too often to the teacher's desk offers a mix of glee and an opportunity for envy to flare.
People stare at the partners and start queuing the hall to the kitchen, expressions tightly controlled.
Tick and Fox head to Cap's office, which is the tidy answer to Grace's disorder. Immaculate, the space is filled with plants. The senior officer's prize orchids huddle in a fragile scrum, shielded from the bright Florida sun. They're surrounded by pebbles and pans filled with water measured to scientific precision.
Cap faces the partners. "Did either of you gentlemen think to call in?"

Fox's jaw slacks, his eyes dropping to the floor. "Sorry. *Mea culpa.*"

"*Mea culpa.* Right." Their senior officer stares them down. "Now would be the next best thing."

Fox fixates on his feet, his go-to separation technique if Brick Breaker is not on hand.

His partner's silence fills Tick with dread. *Oh, man, the medical procedures. He's not going to report anything. Fuck.*

Cap bristles, and the air crackles.

"The vic was dead on scene." Tick, the Knight Errant, swoops in to save. "We ran to the hospital to check some details and were headed right back here. Time slipped past us."

"Yeah, time. Whatever."

Cap hates surprises. He'll blow behind the scenes.

The captain watches Fox, who twists his phone in his pocket and gazes out the window.

Tick scrambles to appear he's not scrambling. He speaks deliberately, drawing the focus from his partner. "The boy's white. Changes some stuff."

"Yes, some stuff. For you two, not much. You still on those paths your wingman told me about this morning?" He jerks his thumb at Fox.

What paths? "Yes, sir. Still, a few critical puzzle pieces are missing. Evidence is coming in. The fog is clearing." Tick's dialect is gone, replaced by the English Lit master's articulate speech.

"You could be the lawyer with that load of crapola, Sergeant Tickman."

"We may have found a connection to a cold case," Fox mutters, eyes glued to the window. His voice interrupts the men. They had accepted he wouldn't join the conversation.

"Cold case?" Cap eyes the lieutenant before glancing out the glass to the empty detective's area. He picks up a file from his desk and examines the pages too carefully for Tick's liking. "Yeah, well. Listen. Let's go to the break room. Missy has a party ready to roll.

She'll be looking for us. Shove off—how do you say it in British? Let's move."

What is this shit? A shock of revelation shoots through Tick. *Fox pulls some weird-ass thing about a cold case, and Cap drops the subject like it's nuclear?* The younger man doesn't keep his face clear of thunder. "Shit is going down, and I'm blocked? What the hell is this?"

Fox ignores both men. His fingers twirl his cell phone inside his pocket, his full attention on the landscaping out the window.

"Come on, sergeant. Let's finish this party thing." Cap shoos the men out the door. "Dr. Argall, move your ass."

They find the detective squad and some deputies crammed into the room and overflowing into the hallway. As the senior officer walks in, everyone scrambles out of the way. Missy, the lead administrative assistant, has laid a cake and pizzas on the table and is holding a wine bottle.

Tick goes to a corner to sulk. Fox pulls out his phone and stays close to the door, as far from his partner as possible.

"C'mon, Miss. We're all here now." Cap smiles brightly at the capable young woman. Missy is going to night school for a psychology degree. She's her boss' favorite, and she uses her advantage.

"No, not me, no sir." Missy steps aside to make room for the captain.

Cap coughs as he finds his place. "We had a major case come together last month. The Bigs and I wanted to acknowledge we appreciate what the effort took and, well, how else to show you except feeding you? The way to a—"

Missy purses her lips. "A *person's* heart is through his or her stomach, right?"

Fox stretches against the counter, legs out, arms crossed. He tilts his head at Cap, suddenly attentive.

"And—" Missy prompts.

"Tick and Fox got commendations, and Miss picked out something or other Tick wanted for his phone or something. And because he's a pain in the ass, or should I say *'arse,'* well, we got Dr. Argall this wine. Because he hates cake. And pizza. Who hates pizza? Cut the cake, Missy. Open the pizza, Matt, before everything congeals."

Missy starts the clapping, and everyone obediently joins in. A few old gruffs scowl at Fox as the young ones stare in awe. Cap waves his hand at the group, and they hustle about for pizza and cake.

Tick, who isn't done sulking, holds his new earbuds and watches Cap carry the wine to his partner.

"A 1991 Colheita." Cap leans back next to Fox, holding the wine for inspection.

The lieutenant raises his eyebrows. "Gosh, wow."

"A great wine, hey?"

Their eyes meet, and Fox hesitates, flinching. "Well, there are no great wines, only great bottles." His cheeks flare.

"We will get through this, *hen gyfaill*. [old friend] We always do."

seven
late lunch—the second day

GRACE WALKS through the strip mall's parking lot to the family-owned Jersey Diner, an Argall family favorite. Fox struggles with eating anything Grace doesn't make, but the owner/chef here is an old friend.

The friends met when the restaurant owner, Kostas Adamos, called in a robbery one night. Fox solved the crime, regaining the stolen money. The family was grateful and wanted to cook for the detective. The chef discovered 'my Dr. Argall didn't eat out,' so he set a goal to win him. After a year of cajoling and allowing the Argalls to witness the meal preparation, the friendship was established.

Fox sits at an outside table, his long legs propped on a chair. He smiles and waves when he notices his wife.

No head in the phone playing. Grace exhales. *A good sign.* She waves back, spotting a wine bottle on the table. "Is the Diner selling wine now?"

He blushes. "Nah, it's mine. Thanks for meeting me for lunch, love." He kisses her full on the mouth and swings her in a circle before setting her down. His eyes shine as he pulls her chair out.

Public affection. Some good news. Grace grins, enjoying the energy. "My pleasure, sweet Lad."

The Ruin of the Watcher

In public, Grace calls her husband 'Fox' like everyone else. In private, her nickname for him is 'Lad,' short for 'Ladislaw.' *He has more names than most. Of course, he does.*

She met him first as 'Ellis.' Long ago.

Grace Dawes met Ellis Argall at Ohio State on the first day on campus. She thought he was a bit arrogant and a bit odd. He was exceptionally handsome and didn't care about women or conquests like other guys. Grace was intrigued by the combination.

Her best friend Beth Wilson told her they met previously at a camp for gifted kids when they were all fifteen. Grace didn't remember the awkward boy.

Ellis was an intellectual snob, basking in his brain, not his appearance. Uncomfortable with any attention, he hung out with the small group in their dorm, but his interest was limited. He was always present and never there. He was intense. Her mom called him 'torrid, with a menacing undercurrent of obsession you can hear if you listen carefully.'

Ellis, super nerd, menacing? Ridiculous. Grace laughed.

He fell for her and made his infatuation clear. She ignored him with the politeness women use to set a 'friend barrier.' His adoration was sweet and crossed no boundaries, so his presence was never a problem.

Before Grace developed feelings for Ellis, she had fallen in love —hadn't everyone?—with the dashing Will Ladislaw from the Middlemarch mini-series adaptation. She'd read the book, certainly. When the BBC released the mini-series, Grace sat with many others and pined for the clueless Dorothea to give in to her heart with the rakish Ladislaw.

Then, one bleak night off-campus in Columbus, Ellis stepped in and protected her and her friend Beth from a dangerous situation. As the girls panicked, he sang to comfort them. In the weird way life happens, she knew in an instant she would always need him. She understood precisely how Dorothea felt when she ran to the hero in the last scene. Casaubon was safe in comparison. *Where was my Casaubon to cover me in protective dullness before she met the hazardous Ladislaw?*

"A pretty bottle," Grace says. "Where did you buy the wine?"

"Not any wine, darling girl. A 1991 Colheita." Fox picks up the port and slides his hand over the glass lasciviously. "One of the sexiest tawny ports ever created! Warm, delicate, full."

"Wow, sounds risqué."

Her husband's lovely eyes twinkle. "Once you've had this, it's hard to go back again."

"Want me to leave you two alone?" Grace giggles as blotchy redness appears on her throat, flowing angrily north to her cheeks. The sun bursts in her chest, and within seconds, she's dripping sweat. She throws off her top blouse, grabbing a glass from the table. A scene flashes through her mind where she dashes the ice water on herself. She settles for gulping.

Fox's incomprehension is replaced by sympathy as he recognizes the signs of a hot flash. He drops his gaze, suppressing a smile.

"I swear, these things take your breath away, and not in a fun way." Grace rises from her chair, her flaming neck and face competing with her red hair. She paces and smiles, embarrassed. "Port gives me a problem every time."

"Shouldn't the hot flash come after you've drunk the port?"

Grace rolls her eyes. "No, I figure the dastardly things are limited, and my goal is to finish my quota as quickly as possible. Just seeing an unopened bottle will do." A cool breeze helps her body return to normal.

A woman approaches, confusion on her young face. "I'm Kelli. Have you ordered yet?"

Geez. I look like a loon. She picks up the menu she knows by heart to cover her fluster.

"Coffee. I want a grilled biscuit, nothing more." Fox glows his patented charm at the girl, tilting his head as he answers. Kelli flushes, pushing her hair behind her ear.

A possessive stab hits Grace. *The girl actually wiggled. He can't help himself. He's Aubade, assigned to bloom the universe of female flowers.* "Yeah, you always say the same thing and end by ordering the omelet Kostas makes for you."

The wife's role is to bring the little gods back to earth. Fox's flirting is a habit he acquired to help him manage his social struggles. The act lost its meaning long ago.

"Oh, yes, my omelet." Her husband's accent lilts as he peruses the menu. "I rarely enjoy omelets. The texture is usually naff. Kosta's eggs are different. I like his potatoes, too."

Grace shakes her head as he repeats what he has said a million times. "Yes, Lad, the Greek omelet. I will take the steak salad and coffee." She smiles at the young woman. The waitress doesn't blush at her.

Fox is on his phone, playing Brick Breaker.

He doesn't notice anything. Except when he notices everything. "Tell me about your port."

"The station gave it to me, the Bigs and Cap, for the murder case last month." Fox glances at his wife and squirms with glee.

"Wow! I may have another hot flash in celebration." Grace leans to him and caresses his jaw. "How did they choose the wine? I mean, who decided?"

"Cap, I suspect." He shuffles in his seat, his head cocked to the side. "I suppose they thought the work was right."

Grace laughs. "Yes, I expect they did."

He's so happy about this. A blessing in the middle of the sexual assault cases. She slips her shoes off and lifts her feet into his lap, wiggling her toes. "Appears at the perfect time, like a lucky bottle."

Fox lifts his eyebrows at his wife and flicks his eyes theatrically at the surrounding tables, which are filled with chattering patrons. Reaching under the table, he takes Grace's bare feet in his hands. He leans forward and whispers, playing at a Scots brogue. "Well, ye are the bonny lassie with experience in luck, we know, and I'm the jammy beggar."

"Come home early, Lad. Meet me by eight, OK? You won the lucky bottle. I'll bring the magic elixir." She wiggles her toes again. "And I'll make your mum's stew."

"Be sure I'll chivvy Tick along. I promise," he purrs in his singsongy murmur as he runs his fingers up her bare leg. "It's been a positive age since you made my stew!"

A shiver rolls through Grace, and she stops his hand. "Lad—"

"My girl," his voice a low rumble. "You started it."

The pair sit quietly in the slight Florida breeze, a rare moment they enjoy until Fox's phone buzzes.

"Charlie wants to see me." He returns the text. "Told her to give me an hour. She wants to update me on the forensic work from the cases."

"I've got news from my end," Grace says. "In the three current cases, I got the consent and the assent for the second child, Deacon. Both the boy and his parents. Also, the third child —the child we lost. His parents agreed. The first boy's family is considering litigation. They declined." Her eyes close, remembering the anger and shock from the first victim's family.

Fox takes his wife's hand and kisses it. "The living boys still have a stake in the game. Anything we do with the lost boy is critical to a successful prosecution. Two are enough to begin. Depends on what we find. We may have to obtain a court order. I hope not. I wouldn't ask without need, Gracie."

"Oh, honey. Your job is to stop this guy, and mine is to help you. Hard to watch their misery."

"Doesn't make the decisions any easier."

"The second youngster on the fifth floor?" Grace asks. "His name is Deacon. He's talkative since he came out of the anesthesia. He's somehow less harmed by everything and able to find a way forward. The first child. I'm worried about him. He's virtually catatonic. He won't speak. His parents aren't together. The father is angry, spitting, and attacking the mother despite abandoning them long ago. He's back and in charge of assigning blame, sadly."

"Guilt is a hard road. Guilt and shame." Fox's eyes darken.

"Pain is one thing. Suffering is entirely different." Her voice shrinks. "When you can't cope with pain, it corrodes you. You suffer. Nothing is available to the first boy to manage the strain. The second boy accepts the pain and denies its right to hold him. He suffers far less."

"This makes sense to me. I'm a behaviorist at heart. Change the thinking, change the behavior, and you can allow healing to begin."

Grace winces. "How does anyone handle this viciousness? Not become enraged at a cellular level?"

"You see as much as I do, pet. We're in different places in the same line. Can't lose faith or become cynical, or we never see the path forward. Failure would be inevitable. Fail the victims, other cops, the system. I would end by failing you, Marley, and my little Theiss." He slumps in his chair, sighing, tapping on his game.

His hidey-hole.

Heavy silence builds between them. Lunch is no longer interesting.

Finally, Grace laughs, easing the silence. "We're a fun lot."

"Well then! Cheers to us." Fox offers his mug.

Grace clanks her iced tea against her husband's coffee cup and pretends to throw an ice cube down her shirt.

"Now, girlie, what a grand idea." Fox drags his chair to his wife and whispers in her ear. "A wet T-shirt contest at the Argall's? Private showing, y'know?"

Grace giggles, pushing him backward. "Like you would stand in a water-soaked shirt beyond a single second. I can hear you now. 'I'm not for display!' That game would be very one-sided."

"Darling girl."

"No way. Pay the bill, rogue. I'm going to work. Eight o'clock, don't forget."

"Forget," he huffs. "Like I could."

eight
late night—the second day

HOURS LATER, Grace sits in the dark on a tufted loveseat by their walnut four-poster bed. The stew sits on the coffee table, cold. The glaring clock says 11:30 p.m.
No call.
The cop's wife understands the late nights and constant interruptions. She fights the endless fear. Opening her purse, she lifts the package with the prescription she filled earlier in the day. The label reads, 'Do not operate machinery while taking this medicine.' She exhales. *Seems I won't be operating any machinery tonight.* She pops a sleeping pill in her mouth.

The dash clock reads 2:00 a.m. as Fox pulls into the driveway. He caught a murder-suicide when he arrived at the station after lunch. He was going to call Gracie, then other things kept his attention, and the evening became the middle of the night in a flash.

A light is on in the front room. *Is she still awake? This trouble with the menopause.* He would take the stress from her if he could.

Unlocking the door, he finds the alarm isn't on. A pungent, meaty aroma fills the room. He goes upstairs to the bedroom, frowning. His wife is sound asleep on the short sofa at the end of the bed, with a rectangular bench set for dinner. *Mum's stew.* She has on a nightgown. *That frilly, thin thing.* A prescription container sits next to the wine glasses. *Ambien.* He scowls. *She hasn't told me anything about a prescription. Is the insomnia so bad?*

Fox slides the bench away and gazes at her. She whimpers and wiggles but doesn't wake. He gathers his lovely, disheveled wife into his arms, feeling his body respond.

God help me.

He shudders and shakes to change the subject in his head as he carries her to the bed. He stands and watches her for a moment before he tucks her in and kisses her forehead.

My darling girl.

The drug. He picks up the green plastic vial. *How ridiculous.* He exhales, placing the bottle on her nightstand.

He clears the cooled food and utensils, carrying everything to the kitchen. Covering the stew with cling film, he puts the container in the fridge. *Can't waste that.*

nine
early morning—the third day

SOMEONE'S CLANGING *a bell and singing, 'The Delta Queen is coming! Our magnificent sternwheeler is navigating to the bank of the Ohio River!' The calliope begins its magical tune. The calliope! It's the summer song, calling the children to join the fairies for a May Day dance. Grace runs to the river, the grass soft against her bare feet.*

Grace's alarm chimes, and she jolts awake. Fox's side of the bed is empty. 6 a.m., and he's already gone. *What time did he come in? Did he come in?*

His covers are yanked up and hauled across his pillow, sheets bunched underneath.

The way he claims to 'make the bed.'

Is there a man alive who can make a bed? Grace sits and inhales before stumbling toward the bathroom like a zombie.

Suddenly, she remembers. *Stew. Port. Ambien.* The table she had lovingly set for the planned luckiness the night before is cleared away. *No sleeping pills. Where's the bottle?*

She goes back to the bed, looking for the drug. The green vial sits on her nightstand. *Did I put the bottle on my nightstand? Did I get into bed?*

She steadies herself and puts the medicine in her purse on the floor below the loveseat. Her head's a fog, and she has no memory after putting out the food.

A shower will help.

Grace is in the shower when the phone rings. *Fox. The phone's on the bed. I'll call him back.*

After she's showered and dressed, she grabs her coffee and heads for the garage. The phone call. She stops at the kitchen table and pulls her phone from her purse. *Marley. Not Fox.* She sticks her earbuds in and dials her daughter as she backs out of the driveway.

"Marls, I'm sorry. I was in the shower. How are you, everything OK? How's Theiss?" Theiss is their beloved granddaughter, her dear Marley's only child.

How distraught Fox was when she told him she was pregnant with Marley. She recalls the conversation like it was yesterday, not almost twenty-seven years ago.

February, 1984, Columbus, Ohio

"You're what? What?" Ellis ran his hand through his unruly hair and stared in disbelief at his petite, thin wife.

"I. am. Pregnant. Pregnant. Pregnant. Wondering how it happens? You were present at the main event, soon-to-be-Dr. Argall."

"I'm not yet a second year, for God's sake. I have two more years of undergrad, med school, internships, fellowships! How *did* this happen?"

Grace cried as her young husband stalked off.

Present Day

If Grace allows herself to think about it, which she rarely

does, she believes Fox—Ellis, then—needed the next decade to accept their new life.

To accept Marley. She refuses to consider this too fully.

Ellis breezed through undergrad early, bio-chem, *summa cum laude*, first in his class. Grace struggled through those years, juggling nursing school, work, and home. When they both graduated, Ellis started medical school at Ohio State, and she went to work.

The med school years were hell, and they're a blank now.

Her husband graduated with a MD/PhD and top honors. His research work and papers were lauded across the globe. Offers rushed in as he sat at home and sulked. He refused to discuss anything. He refused to work. He just sat.

Months later, Grace returned from work at the hospital, and Ellis shoved a paper at her. His acceptance to Ohio State's Moritz School of Law. She hadn't known he'd applied. She returned the paper to him with nothing to say and went to Marley, who was crying in her crib.

Her husband started law school. Upon another honors graduation, he had offers from all the best firms. He told her one day they were moving to Boston.

⸻

"Moms? Mommy?" Marley's voice drags Grace back.

"Oh, sweetie, I'm sorry. Trouble sleeping. Beth gave me a script for Ambien. I took my first dose last night. Maybe a little hungover."

Beth is Grace's gynecologist and Marley's godmother. She shared classes with Fox at Ohio State when she was a biology major, and they were together through med school. *Beth still calls him 'El,' short for Ellis.*

One of Fox's eighty-seven nicknames. Grace laughs aloud. *Of course. One or even two would never be enough.*

"Moms? Ambien? Mom, what dose did you take?"

"How's classes, love?" Grace asks. Marley attends the Miller School of Medicine at the University of Miami. "Still happy?"

"You sound a little woozy, Moms. No alcohol, right? What dose?"

"Gosh, I didn't notice, sweetie. I took one pill. No drinking. Hey, I'm driving. Let me text you the info later, OK?"

"Listen, the indicated dose is too high for most people, and you're tiny. Some people experience nasty side effects. I'll call Aunt Beth."

Oh, perfect. Marley telling Beth how to treat me. "OK, honey. How are you?"

"I'm fine. Josh has a game tonight and wants me to watch him. A night free—"

"Say no more. We keep Theiss? Yay!" *Fox will be over the moon. He adores his Theissey.* A sudden sadness hits Grace. *He adores Theiss. Dotes on her like he never quite got to with Marley.*

"Marls, you talk with Daddy lately?" Grace struggles to push and not push them together at the same time. "He'll want to hear about school."

"Not lately. He's caught the assault case, yes? I'm sure he's *fuego* busy."

Grace smiles at the Spanish. Their family plays with words and languages. They mix and match them, using accents like props. Everything started when Fox demanded Marley learn Welsh.

Argall Home, 1985-1990, Columbus, Ohio

"Welsh is her heritage! She *must* speak fluent Welsh. It's critical, absolutely critical!" Ellis declared.

"No one speaks Welsh," Grace mumbled.

Afterward, her husband would only speak Welsh to their daughter. "If she cares to understand her dad, she'll learn fast enough."

When Marley was six, she came home from school and announced she would only speak Spanish at home. "If you guys care to understand me, you'll learn fast enough. *Dw i'n credu ynot ti*, Daddy!" [I believe in you, Daddy!]

The innocent delight jumped in her daughter's eyes as she mirrored her father. Marley missed the shadow flickering across her dad's face, but Grace didn't. She didn't miss the slight growl in his voice as he answered.

"If you can, I can, *chica*."

Afterward, their international family threw languages, dialects, and slang terms around any way they wanted. Marley would use entirely fake words and wait for anyone to catch on. *An Argall family joke for anyone listening to figure out.*

Present Day

"So amazing, Moms. The connection between cancer cells and bacteria. Who thought? Biology is so crazy complicated and so simple at the same time!"

"Wonderful, Marls." Grace listens to her daughter explaining her immunology class. *Always so excited. About everything.*

Marley was an extreme extrovert from the day she was conceived. Grace's ribs were her first musical instrument. *My lovely daughter. She should be a musician, not a physician. So creative. Her long, slender fingers fly on the piano or violin as she sings in her father's voice.*

She drew incessantly as a child, on herself and everything else. She painted with anything she could smear. Fox would rant.

Argall Home, 1987, Columbus, Ohio

"Creativity is not the same as out of control, Grace!" He would stamp and sulk.

"Our daughter is you, honey," Grace bribed, begging the father to love their child.

"I have never been out of control."

Snotty, prissy. Grace hated when he acted this way. "Oh, yeah? Well, remember who you're talking to, rogue. I've seen you, don't tell me."

Grace felt herself shutting down to her husband as he demanded she choose between him and her child. A man should never make that mistake.

⸻

Present Day

"Mama? Wowza, Moms. I'm calling Aunt Beth. Are you safe for Theiss?" Marley's voice rises into Grace's mind.

"Daydreaming a bit, I guess. Why don't you call your father? He wants to hear from you."

"OK, Mom. Y'know, if Daddy wants to hear from me, he calls."

She's right, of course. Fox is the caller, the connector, the one in control. *I'm being spiteful about the past, about things best forgiven. Get me together, Lord. He's not the same man anymore. He hasn't been the same man for almost twenty years.*

Her daughter's voice pulls her back.

"Theiss and I'll be at your house by two-ish. Is two-ish too soon? Can you let her be at the hospital with you? Do you need to be later?"

"Two-ish is perfect, sweets. I'm looking forward to holding my baby. Bring her to the house." Grace would leave work early and call Fox to tell him.

He'll come home early, too.

ten
morning—the third day

"EZ JUST SENT THE VERIFICATION." Tick holds his phone in front of his partner.

Fox squats at the bent scrub tree, examining the pine needle-strewn ground at the latest crime scene. "Hmm. Give me a minute."

"No new news. You were right, huge freakin' surprise. Meperidine and midazolam. He choked when he vomited with his head tied to the tree." Tick scans the swampy opening, turning to his partner. "What are you looking for, Shay?"

"Well, this is the stage for the crime. Let me think for a minute." Fox ducks below the yellow scene tape and wanders, surveying the area.

"Thick brush. Perma-damp. Pigs and snakes," Tick recites. "To the east, Military Trail and heavy traffic. To the west, Linsmore and quiet neighborhoods in Abacoa."

Fox stretches his arms over his head and groans. "What am I missing? Summarize, Ticker. Say everything out loud for me."

"OK, boss," Tick says, pulling out his tablet. "Our first victim was found tied to a tree on the other side of Indian Creek, an Abacoa boundary road. The second stumbled out at the southern edge of the Loxahatchee Wildlife Refuge near the other end of the county."

"Why come back here? Loxahatchee is an anonymous place." Fox murmurs, pacing a twenty-foot square outside the scene. "I have to think."

"Ah, yes, think, Dr. Argall. Ponder. Don't worry about me. I'll wait here."

"I make you feel like a fifth wheel. You tell everyone, 'My boss has four all by himself.'"

"You actually listen to me?"

The detective tilts his head, raising his dark eyebrows. "Something is not in place. What happened here?"

"What do you mean, what happened? Shay, man."

"I'm missing something. I play the scene in my head and watch for the evidence I have every right to expect—" Fox squints at a white object in the pine needles and crouches, pulling a glove from his jacket. "Ticker, here's a tooth. Wait, not a tooth. A crown. A veneer or a cap. From a front tooth?" He thrusts his hand around in his pocket for a forensic pouch. "Got a bag?"

"Yup, yessir." Tick examines the small object. "A tooth?" The sergeant pulls a bag from Fox's coat pocket and opens it for him. The detective glowers briefly at his partner before dropping the material into the forensic sleeve.

"A full veneer, like a cap." Fox holds the bag to the light and regards the dental material again, flipping to examine every side. "Cracked off somehow." He holds the item close, twisting it. Handing the bag to his partner, he walks toward the car, taking wide steps. "Let's call a team back here, right? Recheck the area. Find my evidence."

"Right." Tick jogs to keep pace, the brush snapping at him as his partner sweeps ahead.

"Know what, Ticker?"

"Yup?"

"Blood on the front surface of the veneer, I'm sure. Let's talk to the boy at the hospital."

"We talked to everyone already. Repeatedly."

The Ruin of the Watcher

Fox stops and turns. "We really didn't. I didn't." His cheeks grow hot, green eyes rimmed in red. "Oh, so thoughtless."

Tick flares. "Man, we did. You did. What do you mean?"

"I skived. Let the whole thing fly past me. I missed the most important part." Fox's handsome face contorts, and he pounds his fist on the car roof. "This kid fought back. He didn't submit. The drugs led me off."

"OK, Shay, settle down. We're on our way. Even Fox the Fabulous can't always be perfect. Man, I've been real easy with you on this one."

Fox flinches, and his eyes darken before he drops his chin, grinding his jaw. When he speaks, he doesn't look at Tick. His voice is dangerously quiet, his accent heavy. "Whaddaya mean easy?"

Anger flushes Tick's face. "Stuff the shit. I'm not stupid. I was in Cap's office, and I heard everything. Something's happening in this case, and I want the story."

The sergeant stares down his partner, who refuses to make eye contact. "Most people avoid me when they're afraid. Hiding something. When you avoid me, you're punishing me. You're withdrawing."

"I do not exclude you. You imagine things." The detective grits his teeth.

"Bullshit. Don't manage me, asshole. Who do you think you are? The only damn man with a brain on the planet? An atlas carrying us freaking sorry-ass idiots on your sagging shoulders? Bull. Shit. Fuck you." Tick wrenches the driver's side door open and throws himself inside.

Fox stands outside the car for a long time, his arms slung over the open door. Finally, he sighs, slumping into the passenger seat beside the younger man. "What is the benefit if I tell you I smell something, something familiar? Do my vague memories help you? Help us?"

"What the hell does that mean? You fucking smell something?

Fucking shit." Tick bangs his forehead on the steering wheel. "You arrogant son of a bitch."

Fox exhales and lays his head against the headrest. "I can't tell you what I don't know."

Tick throws the door open and storms out. He bashes the door shut behind him and hesitates, adjusting his belt holster.

"Ticker."

Without a word, Tick takes off across the school grounds and heads toward the stadium.

eleven
mid-morning—the third day

THE MORNING WHIZZES BY, and Fox hasn't called. Grace doesn't like to bother her husband at work. Normally, if he left early, he would check in. She dials his cell. His phone rings for too long, and she's about to disconnect when he answers.

"Grace. Sleep well?" Clipped and distant.

He only calls me 'Grace when he's fussing.' "Sleep?" *The Ambien.* "Yes, for the first time in months. Beth gave me a prescription."

"Beth?"

Her husband's voice sounds far away, hidden. Behind the familiar glass wall that separates them, the one she's always pounding on to reach him.

I'm not ready for this.

"Of course, Beth. Who else? Marley thinks the dose may be too high." Jostling in his displeasure, she mentions Marley. *Too late to pull back.*

"Marley. She's aware of this... drugging too?"

"Drugging? Oh, my. Fox. What do you mean, 'too'? I got the script yesterday. I spoke with Marley a few minutes ago. You left for work." Grace pauses. "Thanks for making your side of the bed."

A silence fills in between them, and Grace breathes deep.

When it comes, Fox's laugh is brittle. "I'm sorry, Gracie. I'm having a terrible morning. Sorry for taking my irritation out on you."

Not entirely true. He's upset about the drug, but the wall comes down a bit. Grace makes her husband talk first.

"I made Tick mad, and he left me here by Jupiter Middle School," he grumbles.

"So, your goal today is to irritate everyone who loves you? Excuse me. I need to go. I have warning calls to make."

"Well, snap, sistah." Fox tries to imitate his partner. He botches the attempt miserably and makes his wife laugh. "Darling girl. You never fail to enchant me. I really am sorry."

"Is Tick at the baseball fields?" Grace searches for the better person hiding inside her. *Move from the decades of old memories. Forgive him. I haven't.* The past pain flares like a rotten tooth with so many tiny triggers.

"Expect so. Unless he slipped into the locker rooms. I've known him to show his badge indiscriminately."

"Well, find him and tell him to call me. I'll talk with him about how miserable you are when you're skulking about."

"Skulking? Me?"

Grace veers from the softball pitch. "Guess what, old man? I have a little girl coming at two-ish. Can you ditch your partner early and come hug your sweet baby?" She pokes again. "He'll be happy to see your back."

Zing.

Fox met his granddaughter Theiss when she was a minute old: a red, wriggling, sloppy thing. Thrust into his arms to compensate for being left out of the birth. He bonded with her like a duckling imprinting on its mother. One night, he told Grace the closest thing to the lightning bolt he experienced at Theiss' birth was the first time he heard Grace's sparkly giggle.

He always says the baby changed his molecular structure. Molecular structure. "Honey," Grace says. "You call forensics for results on the bacteria you got in the colonoscopy?"

"No. I need to call Charlie. And retrieve my partner if he hasn't joined a baseball team. They take one look at him, and they'll try to recruit him."

"He respects you."

Fox exhales. "Yes. We'll visit the boy—Deacon, right?—at the hospital for a couple more questions. I'll head back to you and Theiss." He hesitates, and Grace can hear his ragged breathing. Then, he voices an afterthought. "Will Marley come? Josh?"

"Josh has a game. Marls is going with him."

"Right. So, I'm off to eat crow, *mea culpa*."

"Lad."

"Eh?"

"Kiss Tick for me." Grace's fairy giggle.

"I missed my luck last night." Fox's voice is almost a whisper.

Here's the real issue—it's about what he expected and didn't get. The sting hits Grace, and she knocks back. "Can you miss your luck? Seems contradictory. Maybe not your luck, after all."

Her harsh words echo in the third person, and her heart sinks. She forces herself to add, "I think the luck was meant for another day, like today."

If he notices her anger, he lets it pass. "And Theiss?"

"She'll be here until after the soccer match. They'll collect her on their way home, close to dark. The game is at their field. They don't have lights. We can drink your lucky bottle." Grace softens. "I'll risk menopausal danger for you, my darling Lad."

"I love you, sweet Gracie. Sorry about the tweaking earlier. The hormone loss. I can't carry anything for you. Can't fight the enemy for you."

"Ellis—"

Fox rushes on before his wife can react. "No, not my job to save you, pet, I know. My job is to protect you; you must give it to me. I'm a mere mortal man. A slave to my testosterone, as you are to your fickle estrogen."

Grace laughs again. *Her Lad, a mere mortal?* "I love you. So glad I never married my Casaubon and wasted any life before you." *Those lost ten years after Marley's birth.*

In silence, they both know what the other is thinking.

"Casaubon might have spared you." Fox doesn't pass the chance to talk aloud.

"He would bore me. Marley would be mostly bald and probably need those little glasses. And his teeth! No mounds of curly black hair and blinking cat eyes. No aching, tear-jerking voice. I'm certain Casaubon couldn't sing."

"No, love, he certainly couldn't sing."

"Right. See? It would never work."

"No."

"Two-ish, remember? Kiss Tick. He's so nice to you. Be nice back, Lad."

twelve
late morning—the third day

FOX CROSSES Frederick Small Road and jogs toward the university. It's a stunning south Florida spring day, clear and 65 degrees. The locals complain and wear sweaters. He shrugs his coat jacket off, then remembers his holster and pulls it back on his shoulder. When he raises his head, he finds Tick across the tree-lined street waiting for him.

"Thought you were meeting me at the fields?" Fox smiles, dropping his eyes.

Roger Dean Stadium is home to spring training for the St. Louis Cardinals and the Miami Marlins. Tick lives for baseball, and Fox likes every sport. Especially rugby, of course. The partners spend as much time at the stadium as possible, but weekends are not off days for police detectives.

"Nah. I was always gonna meet you here." The younger man frowns.

"You took the keys on purpose?" He doesn't have to ask.

"What else, man?"

Their phones sing out simultaneously. Not Cap's ring. Fox's general tone is Twila Paris, and Tick's is a rap.

Fox didn't put the song in. He suspected Marley but never asked.

"John Tickman." Tick walks off to answer.

Fox stops under a tree. "Argall."

"Detective Argall?" A woman's voice, distant.

"This is he."

"Don't you know who the monster is?"

"No, who is this?"

"I mean, don't you know who did those terrible things? Hurt those little boys?"

Adrenaline rushes Fox's chest. "No. Do you?" Pushing his Welsh lilt, he forces nonchalance. His breath catches as instincts kick in. *Is the voice familiar? Female, a bit squeaky, young? A Boston accent?* He taps a quick note of his impressions. He needs tech to get a fix on the caller's GPS.

Find the number. No burner, please. Please.

The woman's voice breaks in, scathing. "Hell, yes, I do. And so should you, of all people on the planet."

The line cuts dead.

Fox hits the call pad and dials tech. "Hey, got a weird call. I need you to run the info. Yes, Lieutenant Argall. Need my cell number? No? OK. Text me everything. Thanks, man." He waves at Tick, but his partner is deep in conversation, so he calls the forensics lab. "Charlie, pet, you got anything for me?"

Charlotte 'Charlie' Perez. She always cheers me.

Charlie and her husband left on an infamous float from Cuba not long after Castro took control. Her husband perished a mile from the shore. The widow pulled herself together and went to school. Got an MS in Forensic Science from the University of Miami, and now she's working on her PhD.

Charlie's stunning. He teased Ez once about the Cuban women. Dazzling, unlike the men. The medical examiner had some explanation about his countrymen and physical proficiencies. Fox pointed out the suggestion made little sense, and Ez just shrugged.

"Detective Dr. Argall. How you doin', *guapo?*" Charlie drawls her accent, a joke between them.

Fox searches his memory for what *'guapo'* means. *Spanish.*

Something Marley said while banging on. "Are you cursing at me, pet?"

"No, *guapo* is beautiful, *besito, cariño,*" Charlie chuckles.

"Oh. Well. I accept." He smiles at the phone. *She's delightful.* "Got the swab back, Detective. The swab, *es ser un punto—*"

"Charlie. English or Welsh, please. My Spanish is rusty. And if you're going for Welsh, speak a little slower. I only talk to my mum once a week."

A few yards away, Tick returns his phone to his pocket and makes his way to his partner. Fox clicks the call to the speaker.

Charlie lets out a belly laugh. "Yes, *asere, si.* Sorry, I don't have Welsh yet. The data confused me a bit, *en la primera. Múltiplo* viral and bacterial pathogenic strains."

"Tick's here, you're on speaker. You say the swabs showed multiple STDs? Can you obtain a match? Verify the molecular structures?"

"*Si.* I can. You have all you want, both boys. I need a standard. I'll give you answers. Track back to the source, friend."

"So, each boy, the same donor. The same infected donor." A rush of heat overtakes him. *I have the bastard. Finally. It's him.*

"*Si.* I need the standard. I'll give you the proof."

"I will, Charlie, lovely lady." Fox disconnects the call. His smile disappears as the tension tightens on his partner's face.

"So you spillin' now, bro?" Tick's six-foot, six-inch frame blocks the sun. He's ready to fight.

"Let's head to Rooney's. I'll fill you in as best I can."

"Not 11 o'clock yet, Shay. Rooney's doesn't open until 4:00 p.m. this afternoon. Le Grenouilles at Metro will have to do."

"La Grenouille. Les Grenouilles," Fox corrects.

"Fuck you, man."

Downtown Abacoa is a crossroads of four roads surrounding Roger Dean Stadium. The streets are dominated by an eclectic mix of small ethnic restaurants and sports bars, including the Pittsburgh Steelers' eponymous Rooney's. Corporate offices line the road across from the storefronts and circle the grassy Florida Atlantic University Honors College campus.

The Abacoa developers imagined a bustling social scene supported by major league baseball, with the hometown Marlins and the winning St. Louis Cardinals spring training at the stadium. Instead, they ran headlong into the easy real estate money market crash in 2008. Even during the day, the downtown is nearly vacant, with darkened, unleased buildings and empty streets.

Black and white, like an old photo. Tick loves the quaint area despite the often barren landscape. *The town is comfortable, familiar. The Argalls make it feel like home. Grace welcomes him the same as family. We are family.*

The two men sit outside at the French bistro Les Grenouilles, waiting for service. Tick loves their roast beef sandwich. Fox avoids eating anywhere unless Grace makes the food.

Tick squirms in his seat, watching Fox and fighting his growing anger. His partner is faded somehow, straight from the rumpled photo, washed out to grayscale. *Time to man up.* He leans back in his chair, crossing his arms. *I won't make this easy. He has to speak first.*

Fox's eyes drop to his phone, which sits on the table. His fingers inch forward, stroking the device.

Brick Breaker. His drug. The wheels spinning through Fox's head show in the gathered brows and lowered chin. *Will he tell the truth?* Tick exhales. *At least the part he decides to dole out.*

"OK. You remember the pin?" Fox glances past Tick, his gaze unfocused.

"The freaky old lady pin. Yeah." Tick doesn't trust him yet.

"Those stones. They're real. The pin is worth thousands."

"So?" Tick spits on the concrete sidewalk. His partner detests anything vulgar. He watches as Fox blinks, hollow-eyed. *Good as a flinch for prissy Dr. Argall.* "How is this pin related to our cases?"

The detective shivers, stammering, "I didn't—I don't, not for sure. I didn't chuff you off."

Tick suppresses a smile. 'Chuffing off' is a curse coming from Fox Argall. 'Old Man' Martin warned him when he drew Fox as a new partner.

"He don't cuss, man, hates pizza. What the fuck? Total weirdo. Not normal. A foreign fancy-pants smart-ass Jesus freak. Emphasize freak. He'll get you killed. Dump him fast."

The sheer antipathy toward the unusual man from the other cops first made Tick dig in. And he hasn't regretted his decision. As pissed as he is now, Fox Argall is the best draw in his career.

"So, you weren't sure. Now, time to share." Tick spits again.

Fox taps his foot under the table, eyes darting from left to right. Any other day, Tick would love this vulnerability. Today, everything the guy does pisses him off. He squares his jaw and crosses his arms, waiting.

"Twenty years," Fox sighs. "Crazy."

Tick lets the man take his time, watching his partner's face wrench. He controls a stab of pain at his friend's anguish. *I've never seen emotion from him. Not like this.*

"October 1991. Marley was turning seven." Fox inhales and clears his throat. "I was working at a huge law firm in downtown Boston. Grace had a birthday party, and you just had to have the partners and associates and whatever." His chest heaves as he pulls in a breath. "One of my senior partners came to Marley's party with a man I'd never met. A strange, strange man. My partner insisted I meet the man in my library and talk. The man was a friend, my partner said. A client. He was going through a rough divorce. His wife wanted more money than he wanted to give. Could I help? I'm a healthcare lawyer, I say. I wanted nothing to do with this man. I recoiled at the thought. A visceral reaction."

He's breathing through his mouth. Panting. "Settle, Shay. We'll be fine. We're going to manage this."

"My law partner laughed at me, threw me under the bus. 'You graduated *summa* from Ohio State with an MD/PhD. Your doctoral dissertation is on DNA, right? Molecular genetics? I think you can handle everything,' he said." Fox groans. "Handle what? A divorce?"

Tick swallows hard. Fox is a freak. *What is he doing playing cop in south Florida?*

The air is still and oppressive, and the sun is growing hot. Tick leans forward into his despairing partner. "Time to tell me the story. The whole thing. Stop shutting me out. This is not about you, man. There are broken and dead children here."

"You're right. You're right. Such an old and ugly story." Fox shifts in his seat, his fists white-knuckled. "Yes. This started 20 years ago at my home in Boston, at Marley's birthday party. I was 'Ellis's to everyone then."

thirteen
october 2, 1991, boston

THE ARGALL RESIDENCE
Agassiz, Cambridge, Massachusetts, 1991

"Who needs to hear me play my violin?" A jubilant Marley pulls on her mother's arm, passing the table piled with brightly colored presents. She ignores her lovely pink cake, with the buttercream flowers piled on as Grace wanted. "I got a new violin for my birthday, a real-sized one!"

At only seven, Marley is almost five feet tall, graduating from a child-sized instrument to her first adult version. Performing in her life to an unseen audience, the little girl shines with a vigor unknown to either parent.

Ellis watches Marley from the expansive tiled patio in their backyard in the brick-lined leafy enclave of Agassiz, Cambridge. Rented chairs and tables fill the space, each topped with ice buckets, wine, and glittering glasses.

My daughter is persuaded everyone must share her life at all times. Hearing the little girl call out for an audience, he shivers. *This uncontrolled energy is so unseemly. The unrelenting demands are selfish. Clutching.* His feelings about his only child circle him every day. He tells himself he wins more often than he loses.

Grace invited simply everyone to the birthday party. Ellis dreads hosting his business colleagues at their home. *Chaos in my sanctuary. My free time should be my time. But there it is. Politics.* A headache threatens. He arranges his face to pleasantly neutral for the adults staring at him. *The host.*

Marley's lyrical voice—a siren's call—streams back into Ellis's consciousness. "Daddy!"

"Marley, Marls, let's wait until everyone has their cake. They can listen to you while they eat." Ellis struggles to hide his irritation.

"While they eat? Oh, Daddy!" Marley guffaws. "How silly! How can they dance if they're holding cake?" She falls forward, giggling.

The adults drop their heads in unison, laughing. Heat flies up Ellis's neck. *Nothing new with my girl.* His attempts to smile end in a grimace as he looks helplessly at Grace. His wife rejects the silent request by focusing her attention on their daughter.

"Marley has practiced a jig for our Boston friends, Ellis," Grace says. "She's going to do 'Rose in the Heather.' She's sure they'll want to dance."

"Daddeee! Daddy, here's the best idea ever! You play with us! We'll do Promenade. I'll do the slip jig! Or you sing 'Danny Boy.' You're so fabulous at ballads, Daddy. You can sing, and I'll play for you. I'll get your guitar." Marley skips off.

Ellis is steaming. *Why didn't I prepare for this? I should expect Marley's behavior and Grace's refusal to help. Everyone is watching me. Calm, stay calm. All I can do in this turmoil.*

"Well, Dr. Argall, your musical talent was unknown when we hired you. 'Danny Boy' would land you an extra percentage anywhere in Boston." Tom Masters is a senior partner at Ellis's office. "Do Welshmen sing the Irish anthem?"

"This Welsh son sings the song beautifully," Grace murmurs.

Where is the help to escape?

Marley larks back, holding hands with an older man carrying a guitar.

Ellis waves his hand toward his old friend and his daughter. "Well, here comes The Voice, ladies and gentlemen. Meet Marley's Uncle Roofie and his famous 'Lovely Yamaha' FG730S acoustic."

Roofie glides up, pulled along by the excited birthday girl. "Is our host telling you he can't sing if I'm in the same state?"

"A tad cynical, to my hearing," Ellis murmurs.

The adults on the patio laugh and erupt with yeses.

"Don't let the man fool you. I'm merely the tenor to his baritone." Roofie grins at his friend. "This one prefers his talents to remain as hidden as possible."

Beside himself, Ellis shuffles in an odd dance. He's gone from trying to maintain control of the party to trying not to lose it in front of his entire law firm.

Marley stares at her father with quiet, challenging green eyes. *My eyes.*

"You will be OK, Daddy. 'Danny Boy' is not a duet. Uncle Roofie will wait for his turn."

Ellis can barely think to speak. The blackness rolls in, threatening panic. "Really, Roof, how can you stand there and say without a lightning strike that a baritone should perform a tenor masterpiece? While you're in the room?"

Roofie locks eyes with him, a warning in his calm gaze. "OK, tell you what. I'll do 'Danny Boy.' Birthday girl still gets to play and sing with her daddy. She has other songs. The birthday wish, Dad."

Nausea floods him. *This has gone off the rails.*

Marley leaps into the air. "Daddy! Uncle Roofie can sing the song! He practiced with me last night. He can slay this one! I helped him."

Grace laughs; her fairy tinkle. "Uncle Roofie sure can slay this one." She moves to her husband and leans against his arm. "Right, honey?"

"Yes, *fy merch* [my daughter]. Roof can bring our hearts to our throats." He forces himself to relax.

Marley throws her hip to the left and claps her hands, staring her dad down with dancing eyes and her most charming grin.

"How much is this girl her father's child?" Grace rubs Ellis's arm. The adults chuckle at the spectacle, which includes the father's flushed face.

"I would have insisted on an Argall party long ago to experience this side of our good doctor." Tom winks at the group.

Numbness replaces the engulfing darkness as Ellis regains some calm. "OK, I can't keep anyone from hearing Roofie sing anything, much less 'Danny Boy.' Marls, you ready with the violin? This is a hard one, *calon bach* [small heart]."

"*Ymddiried ynof*, Daddy! Trust me! We got this, don't we, Uncle Roofie?" Marley beams at her beloved uncle. Suddenly, she yells. "Wait! Aunt Beth! Wait! *Aunt Beth*! We're going to sing! Come, come!"

Beth leans out of the open kitchen door. "Marls. Settle, chick. Too much chocolate." She comes out, wiping her hands on her pants. She places her hand on the child's head and smiles at the gathering.

"Dr. Beth Wilson, Marley's godmother," Ellis says. Beth and I attended medical school together. She's visiting for my daughter's birthday—apparently, a national event." He flicks his hand at the child. "Go, my darling girl."

Marley's face grows serious as her uncle readies the guitar. She rolls the violin on her small shoulder and waits for his signal. Roofie nods to the little girl, and his voice fills the space, moving out into the neighborhood. His magical voice transfixes everyone. Roofie locks Marley into his gaze as he sings, and she doesn't miss a note. Tears always come with the plaintive 'Danny Boy.'

A most appropriate song. Ellis's friend Patrick McNeill, a client's chief in-house counsel, committed suicide two weeks ago after a legal case went sideways for him. *Life is too complicated for some people.* He closes his eyes and listens. When he reopens them, he spots a peculiar man standing apart from the group, staring at him.

Who is this? The lone man stands by the gate in the backyard. A younger man with a bulging shoulder holster and an earpiece hovers nearby. *A bodyguard? Who brought a bodyguard to my child's party?*

The odd man nods, motioning toward Ellis. He smiles at his companion, and his face splits like a snake shedding its skin.

Ellis shudders. *Who is he?*

The guests break into applause for Marley's impromptu concert, interrupting Ellis's thoughts. Tom Masters raises a hand, waving at the two strangers across the grass.

Tom brought these men?

His partner makes his way over, tapping his shoulder. "Ellis, El— Listen, can we meet in your study for a minute? I got someone for you to meet and want to run down something quick."

No real surprise. Tom invades my child's party with work. Irritation floods him. *Yet, avoiding a musical performance by pleading work? A bonus.* His thoughts are flying in every direction. *Pull yourself together, man.* "Sure. Let's talk in the library, through the double glass doors." Ellis passes the acoustic back to Roofie, pointing to the house. He searches for Grace. She's watching Marley entertaining everyone with fiddle runs.

Ellis heads through the French doors opening into his library. Roofie flicks his head at him as he walks into the house, tilting his head at the bizarre man and the bodyguard. Ellis rolls his wrist and fingers in their private 'I'm OK' signal.

Dark bookshelves cover the expansive room. A cherry writing desk sits on an antique Persian rug.

Tom holds a book. "Zane Grey first editions? These are classics."

"I got my first one from my dad when I was twelve. I love westerns." Ellis cocks his head to the side. "Zane Grey is the best. I lived close to Zanesville, a small town near Columbus when I attended Ohio State. I trolled the second-hand stores for seven years."

Tom's voice rises in surprise. "The same Zane?"

"Yes. The family were English Quakers who came in the 1600s and settled in the Philadelphia area—across the river in New Jersey. Little town called Collingswood. Zane Grey's ancestors moved to southeast Ohio."

Ellis catches himself tunneling into a monologue. His cheeks flush pink as he pulls himself out. He strains to keep his fingers from fluttering.

"Zanesville, no." Tom stares at Ellis's hands, smiles, and looks down. "Collingswood, yes. I'm from south Jersey. Amazing. These are beautiful."

The familiar, self-righteous 'I understand your struggle' smile. Ellis has seen the same expression a thousand times. *You know nothing. You will never know.*

A tap on the glass breaks the tension. The odd man has pushed the door open but hasn't stepped inside. "Sooo much knowledge. Such a rooom. How impressive." The voice is a low hiss.

"Senator Conway, please come in," Tom says. "Let me introduce you. This is Ellis Argall, MD, PhD, JD."

"'Conway' is Welsh," Ellis notes. He clasps his fingers behind his back to avoid any attempt to shake hands.

The man leans to his left and winks, making clear he noticed Ellis's movement. "Yes, as is 'Ellis Argall,' my educated friend. The lovely accent."

"Yes," Ellis mumbles.

"Excuse me, I never shake hands," the senator giggles, winking again. Conway grins his troubling snake smirk, and Ellis's blood thickens.

He's teasing me. What a sad excuse for a smile. Ellis glances at Tom. His partner has a vacant grin plastered on his face. *No help from him.* "It is Welsh, mate. Deep in the heart."

"When did you arrive in the U.S., Dr. Argall?"

"Please, call me 'Ellis.' Early 80s, on a student visa. I became a citizen during medical school."

"I'll never neglect to address you properly, Dr. Argall. This *in-tell-i-gence*. Those long years of school. I suspect you were so very young, a sweet thing. Am I right?" Conway leers, playing with the words. "The United States is a blessing, bringing such—fascinating people. People like you from everywhere in the world."

Senator Conway's face cracks open again.

An ogle, he's gloating. Ellis covers a shiver by picking up a letter opener. "The United States is a blessing to me." He meets the man's eyes for a single second. *Glee. He's enjoying my discomfort.* "I knew my life would play out here, not in my beloved Wales."

Tom clears his throat. "Senator Conway has a legal need, Ellis. You will be helpful. Specifically helpful."

Ellis's breath snatches away, like in the children's fable of the cat. "How can I help?" He steadies himself and calls on the years managing his reactions, masking. *Cover it.*

"Senator Conway is going through a nasty divorce. His wife is vindictive." Tom strolls to another shelf, and the room swims with an indefinable conflict. "Senator and Mrs. Conway have a daughter who is Marley's age," he continues. "Mrs. Conway is threatening to accuse the senator of child abuse. A litigation tactic. The daughter and some schoolmates. We agreed you can help."

Panic shoots through Ellis. *I'm overreacting. Peace, man. Relax.* "I'm a healthcare lawyer." He forces a charming smile. "I worry about the agency—the FDA—and whether your counterparts in DC will mess with Medicare this year. I haven't been in a criminal courtroom since I was a student. Never worked a divorce."

"Any case would be in a divorce process, yes, if anything. Which I sincerely doubt," Conway snickers. "Dr. Argall. I understand you're a physician."

"I studied and taught medical research, Senator. I never practiced medicine." Ellis hates the catch in his voice. "I'm not a practicing physician."

"You hold a PhD with top honors in cellular biology and an

official medical degree," the strange man sneers. "Top honors, all around, the very highest. You keep your medical license up to date in Ohio and Massachusetts."

"Yes—" Ellis stammers.

Conway fixes his stare on him. "Quite the impression your doctoral dissertation made, Dr. *Arrgaall.*" Conway drawls on the name. "Published in Molecular Genetics. The talk of the season, yes? Still used in biopharmaceutical research. The basis for new agents, *yesss?* Everyone wants you, dear. Everyone who meets you falls in love."

Conway's voice is silky, like petrol.

"Yes. Yes," Ellis rambles, reeling from the bizarre man. *There's much more to this than divorce.* Fighting a creeping fear, he flashes a look at his senior partner. Tom is studying the Zane Grey first editions as though his life depends on memorizing them.

"I have some medical challenges, Dr. Argall. Resistant forms of *chlamydia trachomatis* and human *papillomavirus*. You're the expert, Doctor. Both are challenging to treat." His voice lowers, and he smirks. "Can't you test the children and prove I didn't— touch them? I mean, if I had, wouldn't they have my stamp?"

Oh, God. What a repulsive point. Everything about this guy is repugnant. Ellis settles his voice but can't raise his head. "Yes, they may. They might." He leans his palms against his desk, staring at the blotter. "It is possible to contract the infections if no protection was used."

"So, you can track the author?" Conway chuckles. "For those particular stories? Am I right?"

Red fury hits Ellis and rolls down his spine. "I don't consider any variation of the scenario amusing, Senator." He can't tear his eyes off his desk pad.

After a hesitation, Conway's voice is like lead. "Of course not, Dr. Argall. Certainly not. Excuse my stress reaction. Horrible to contemplate."

Tom shifts from the bookshelves to listen. "Goodness," the senior attorney says. "This is so frightful. How would anyone find the right way to think, much less talk, about such a subject? Dr. Argall will be glad to handle this medical issue. We will vigorously defend you against these scurrilous charges. Extortion, plain and simple."

Bile rushes into Ellis's throat. *How is Tom supporting this?* Conway's eyes never leave him. "Dr. *Arrgall*. You seem disturbed. What are you *thinnking*?"

The weird drawl.

Anger overwhelms him as his opinion of the man hardens. "I wonder whether these children's parents would agree to the requisite testing. We may need a court order."

Tom brightens. "Our specialty, El."

Good grief, Leona. To stop from groaning, he adds, "I can talk with Grace. She'd be familiar with any voluntary process. I don't see a simple path to this." He instantly regrets his brash words.

The senior partner relaxes, smiling at Ellis's mention of his wife. "Dr. Argall's better half, Grace, is a PhD candidate in Bioethics at Harvard, Senator Conway."

Why did I bring Grace into this? Tom is reading acquiescence. Nausea roils in his stomach, driving saliva into his mouth. He swallows hard, stifling the urge to shuffle. He lifts his gaze to Conway's amused smile.

"Oh, my. *Grace*. Another Argall doctorate. You collect them, *yesss*? How totally educated. How very *lovely*. You Brits like the word 'lovely,' right, Dr. Argall?" Conway simpers and laughs before pretending to cough.

When he says, 'Dr. Argall,' he strokes the words. An out-of-body feeling swamps Ellis. *This man never blinks. My God. Like a character from a book. This can't be real.*

Conway's eyes are locked on Ellis, and the senator laughs again. "You're too pretty to be so shocked, dear boy. I wouldn't worry about a judge's order. It won't be a problem." His face splits in scorn. "You have your work, Dr. Argall, and I have mine."

A lively song grows louder outside the door, and Marley bursts into the library with a scream. "Dad! Daddy? Uncle Roofie is playin'. He's playin' and says, "Where is El-lis Argall?" The child giggles and pounces on her father's legs.

Ellis plucks her into his arms and strides to the French doors, kissing her solidly on the forehead. "Scoot, Marls, scoot. Daddy is working." He searches the stone porch to catch Roofie's eyes.

Roofie comes over, grabs Marley's hands, and swings her in the air, eliciting excited screeching from the little girl. "Come, Marley-girl. Dad will be with us in less than ten minutes." He stares his friend down.

Ellis nods. "Less than ten minutes." Turning to Tom and Conway, he says, "I'll complete the memo by late Monday. Can you send me the records by tomorrow?"

"Everything by first light tomorrow." Tom pats Senator Conway's arm to lead him out of the library and back to the patio. "Let's find out what Grace is cooking. She's a marvelous cook."

Conway follows Tom from the library, passing Ellis. At the last minute, he slips his hand out and touches Ellis's arm, lightly scratching his hand with long fingernails.

"I'll be with you in a sec, Tom," Ellis says, shaking. As he puts the Zane Greys back in alphabetical order, someone presses into him from behind, fast and hard. He struggles to turn against the solid wall of the bodyguard, finally throwing the intruder on the thick carpet.

Soft laughter fills the room. "Dr. Argall, I'm so sorry." Conway's bodyguard sniggers as he rises to a sitting position and then stands. "Didn't mean to spook you. Hey, such a glorious child. What do you call her? Marls? How adorable. Love the name. Can't keep your eyes off her, can you? I'm sure nobody can." The man leans forward and shoves Ellis against the bookshelves, jeering. "Glorious."

The rage explodes again, and this time, Ellis can't regain control. "You bloody wanker. I don't care who you are. I don't care about your boss." Lifting the man off the ground, he slams him into the wall, splitting his lip. Blood smears the white paint as the bodyguard slides to the carpeted floor.

The stranger chokes, unable to find breath.

"If you ever threaten my child or my family again, I'll shave your skin off your body." Ellis yanks the man to his feet and flings him toward the doors. "I know how to hurt you, and I will."

The man lands on his knees and his forehead hits the French door. He coughs and spits blood on the glass. "Oooh, Dr. Argall. Con—Senator Conway will be so sorry to miss this testosterone." He stands, dusting off his trousers. "You have a dilemma, Doctor. Time to decide where you stand."

The Argall's backyard is finally quiet. Marley's party is over, and Roofie and Ellis sit by the firepit off the patio in the fading light.

Thank the Lord the other guests are long gone. "I'm so glad this is over." Ellis draws in a ragged breath. "I'm desperate for silence."

Beth, Roofie's wife Stella, and Roofie's mother Mary are helping Grace settle Marley for bed. It's always a monumental task requiring multiple workers.

"Who were those men the Masters gent took into your library?" Roofie asks.

"Tom's friend." Ellis's face clouds. "A nasty divorce."

"You a divorce lawyer now?"

Ellis squirms, crossing his legs.

"You need to take care with your tell. I would kick your butt if I were a gambling man. I might take you on, anyway. Dear friend. Do I dig into your work, ever?"

"No." Ellis stares into the fire, flexing his jaw.

"Did I mess with you when you walked off from a medical degree, sat around, and went to law school without notice? Threw off on Grace to support you another couple years?" Roofie leans back into his chair, folding his hands into his lap.

"No." The flames jump and flicker across Ellis's stoic face as he runs his fingers through his hair.

"We trust each other, yes? Am I the only one who thinks this is family here?"

"No," Ellis sulks. He remembers Grace's face the day she came in from a double nursing shift, and he handed her an acceptance letter to Ohio State's Moritz College of Law. His beloved wife's expression went from surprise to anger in seconds. The guilt is a sharp pain in his stomach, even now.

"El. We can't change the past. God doesn't care about where we've been. He doesn't care where we are right now. He cares where we choose to go. Where are you going?"

"I'm trying to provide for my family. Do my job. I report to people who tell me what to do."

"So, now we do what we're told?" Roofie laughs and shakes his head. "Ellis Argall."

"I let Gracie down." Ellis stands and paces by the firepit, shuffling in his awkward dance. "I laid off on her for over five years. Time to be a grown-up boy."

"Does Grace understand why you walked away from medicine?"

In the years following his graduation from medical school, the friends have never discussed the subject.

Not after the first day. The first terrible day. Ellis slams himself back into his chair and slumps with his head back, eyes reddening. "How could I talk to her? Not about this."

"How could you *not* talk? How has this omission affected your relationship?" Roofie leans toward his suffering friend. "We make decisions. Some are good, some not-so-good. Truth heals. An omission, rejecting truth, is a lie. Lies can be silent, and they destroy just like the spoken ones. They create division. No excuses can change a toxic reality, but talking out loud brings healing."

Tears stream down Ellis's face. The words he wants to speak are stuck in his throat. He drops his head into his hands.

"Ellis, I love you." Roofie squats before the fire, his back to his friend. "My brave, faithful brother. Talk out loud to your wife about this."

"Brave and faithful? Brave and faithful. She hates me."

"Nonsense. She loves you with her entire being. You're acting like a child about this. You made a mistake. You learned and grew. What else can anyone ask?"

"You didn't see her that day."

"That day is gone. Your wife is another person, as you are another person. If you'd stood against the lies you heard in your spirit, you and Grace—and Marley—would have this behind you. Time doesn't heal a festering wound, right, Doctor? Some healing requires surgery, right? You need to cut some things out?"

"How do you cut evil from your soul?" Ellis whispers, and the echo blasts inside his brain.

"Are you implying others don't have evil in their souls?" Roofie stares at his friend. "Look at me. Remember the first time we spoke? I had a stolen gun in my waistband, and I was planning on hurting Grace and Beth after I scared you off. And enjoying my time. I would have used the gun. I *had* used the gun. You speak to *me* of evil in one's soul?"

"Roof."

"Forgiveness is real, El. It's a miracle healer." Roofie leans toward the fire and drip-feeds another wood slice into the flames. "Where we're going right this moment is what matters. It's what our God cares about."

"I wanted Grace—I wanted to kill my baby. I wanted to kill Marley. Violate my oath to do no harm."

"Nonsense. You wanted an easier life because you were frightened. Many are frightened, and many seek a simpler way."

"Death, not life, nonetheless. Not worthy of Hippocrates."

"You and I had the same goal, same as many others. Make our lives easier," Roof repeats. "The world's choices. I'm not reducing anything. Don't focus on one foolish choice or a foolish time in the past. Don't trap yourself inside a poison prison. Talk out loud. Move forward."

Ellis sits with his head in his hands, his feet tapping.

"Repentance is turning around and going the opposite way.

Have you repented for rejecting Marley? Face the pain, friend. Where are you headed? If you don't change direction, you'll end up where you're going." He pauses. "OK, enough. This Conway fellow? The man is trouble. Major trouble, I suspect, beyond what you and I have seen. And we have seen trouble."

"The senator needs some DNA tests." Ellis pulls his gaze from the flames, focusing on his shoes. "To check for pathogens. Diseases. DNA origins for venereal diseases Conway contracted. Sexually transmitted diseases. Highly resistant to treatment. His estranged wife is accusing him of abusing his daughter and her friends. He wants to prove he didn't assault the children."

Roofie inhales, tossing another log to the fire from the pile beside his chair. "The man's a senator?"

"A state senator from Boston."

"Will the tests prove these assaults?"

"If he assaulted them and used protection, they might not rule him out. Absence proves nothing. He wasn't appalled or embarrassed. Or scared. He seemed amused. Enjoying himself. Baiting me or something. Like my irritation thrilled him. He was —I dunno." Ellis scowls, accent thick. "I understand nothing. Nothing."

"I think you do understand. However, your point is well taken. What will you choose?"

"After Tom and the senator left the room, his bodyguard snuck in behind me. Naff. A lark for him. He said Marley's 'glorious.' A threat. I put him into a wall. Warned him. What is this, Roof? What do you think this is?"

"I see everything exactly as you do. You're a perfectly intelligent human being with excellent instincts. It's a power play. A man used to winning. You're a challenge. Was the man threatening Marley or you?"

"Both—Both." Ellis remembers the bodyguard's last words: 'Decide where you stand, Doctor.' He doesn't mention the interaction to his friend. He can't say it out loud.

No one gets to threaten my family.

fourteen
late morning, continued —the third day

LE METRO, **Abacoa, present day**

Fox's eyes drop to his phone, but he doesn't reach for it. "The bloke's name was—is—Conway. Conway is a Welsh name." His face jerks in pain.

"OK. What else?" Tick attempts to sound harsh and fails. "C'mon, you're doing good."

His partner tilts his head and stares past Tick, his eyes unfocused. "His diseases were highly resistant to treatment. He stood there, cool as cucumbers, and asked to test the children and prove he didn't abuse them. Prove they didn't share the same diseases."

Jagged breathing fills the silence.

A breeze blows leaves in a mini-tornado toward their table. The partners watch the whirlwind for too long.

"Turmoil. It's a sign. Emblematic of my soul." Fox's jaw slackens, and red splotches form on his face.

Tick inhales and slowly blows his breath out. The metal chair presses into his thighs, and he shifts in a vain attempt to find comfort. "What did you do? When the guy asked you to help?" He looks a decade older than yesterday. *I've never seen him with any genuine emotion, much less this suffering.*

"Grace was at Harvard at the time, getting her PhD," Fox repeats and falters. "I was looking for a way out, so I used her. I claim to love her and race off, using her to save me. Failed in involving her." The detective shivers violently.

Did Grace get hurt by this weird senator? Tick's shoulder cramps, and he flexes his fists under the table to relax.

"I asked her about the ethical concept for the tests. Frantic for a way out, I suppose." Fox's lilt is so strong his words sound blurred. "She said she'd need to research the ethics, and the legal standard was clear. Legally, a court order from a judge would force any kids to be tested. She would expect a fight unless the parents agreed, which didn't appear likely."

He's rambling. "And?"

"Long story short, I obtained the orders, and the kids were infected, but not with the same strains as Conway. Some were HIV positive." His voice lowers to a whisper. "A nightmare." He covers his mouth with his hands. "The parents' horror. The tiny girls no one wanted to think about." His eyes redden and flood again.

Tick exhales, rolling his neck.

"Conway's daughter had HPV in her throat," Fox continues. "The warts had to be treated to keep her airway from closing. Long story short, Conway didn't commit the acts; it was a camp counselor where the kids went. The abuse had gone on for years."

"Not him?" Tick snarls.

"Not directly. We had another culprit, unmistakably guilty. We found no physical evidence to connect to Conway. Couldn't prove anything."

Anger crawls up Tick's spine and twists his face. "So, the guy kept his money?"

"Yes. I didn't handle the divorce, y'know. I was at the firm's offices when they finalized the settlement." Fox slumps forward. "The wife leaves, crying. Conway presses in behind me in our coffee area. Presses in. It's a gigantic room with a full kitchen and a black-and-white checkered floor. One of those fancy colored stoves, y'know the kind? It was always cold in that place."

"Fucking bastard."

Fox rubs his fists together and shivers. "Conway stood so close to me, I couldn't move without hitting him. I froze for a second, and he hissed in my ear: 'Like I would ever touch a girl when I could have Ganymede.' I forced myself around. Had to muscle him back. 'Whaddya mean?' I asked. But I knew. He smiled like a serpent and walked off. He was a pedophile. He just liked boys."

"Ganymede. The cupbearer of the gods." Tick forces himself to sit back in the metal chair. "How's this connected to the pin?"

"Well, I confronted the senior partner. He told me the entire thing was my word against the client's, and I better keep quiet. We had a huge, loud row. I resigned." Fox's jaw clenches, the muscle pulsing like a heartbeat. "It was the talk of the firm. As I was packing my office, a junior admin came in and dropped a file on my papers. The labs from the court order and an inventory of the valuables from the couple. The notations gave the wife the family jewelry. Everything. Had to be millions of dollars. A diamond tiara. Conway even gave her his platinum wedding ring. Everything except this valuable pin. Unique. Rare stones. Been in his family for some time."

"A weird old lady pin."

"Yes." The detective covers his face with his hands. "I didn't remember clearly last week. The memory is so vague. In the horror of the children's pain, I barely registered the inventory. I had to go to my files and look to make sure. When I found the pin in the swamp, at the scene, the thought stuck and wouldn't leave. I realized the stones were real, and I remembered. You understand I had to keep my thoughts to myself until I could suss it?"

Tick growls in his throat and shakes his head. "No, Shay, I'm a detective too. I can detect. Also, my case."

"Yes. Well." Fox flips his phone in a circle. "I kept the labs on him. A clear violation of several state and federal laws. Completely inadmissible."

"Kept his lab reports?" Rage fills Tick, and he squeezes his fingers into tight fists in his lap. "They *fucking* match the boys."

Fox moans and slides sideways in his chair, crossing and uncrossing his legs. "Yes, by my review. I haven't given the Palm Beach lab his sample information. My possession is unethical. I shouldn't have the evidence."

"Un-*fucking* ethical? What about *raping* kids? *Killing them*? What's fucking *ethical*?" Tick's face contorts.

"Ticker, please." It's almost inaudible. He lifts from his seat to stand and sits back down, his mouth twisted. "It's a broken chain of custody. How do I explain where I got the reports? Why do I have possession? They would throw everything out in court. Nothing good can come from bad. A seed grows its own kind."

"I know. *Damn, fuck*. I know."

Fox clears his throat and swallows. "Another thing. The HPV infection in the Conway girl? It was new. Contemporaneous to the divorce. One day, she was late to school, and the nurse called to say the child was hysterical. She reported she'd been kidnapped and assaulted. The physician suspected she had been drugged. Couldn't isolate the agent. Too coincidental for me. To me, the new infection felt like a plant."

"A plant? Like someone assaulted a little girl—Conway's own daughter? To cover Conway's tracks? Oh, man. Oh, man." Tick rocks in his seat, not sure who he wants to beat. Glaring at his partner, a sudden realization hits. *He's haggard, hunched across the table. Pathetic. Thrashing him would be anti-climactic.*

"Yes, purposeful, to mislead the case. Why would anyone take such a risk knowing about the investigation?" Fox groans, dropping his head into his hands. "The situation was complex, beyond the camp kids. Everything fell apart—"

"Fell apart? Shay, man, help me out. You got the guy?"

"Yes, we got the camp counselor, but don't you see? Can't you see?" Fox moans and rocks in his chair. "The connection between Conway and this other... animal. He worked for Conway. I couldn't find evidence. No emails, no text instructions.

We couldn't find the nexus to show collusion. There is no medical evidence that Conway was abusing those kids."

"Well, we're going to find the fucking connection." Tick smashes his palm on the top, bumping the metal table sideways.

"Ticker. Listen. During the following years, I got these notes. Sprayed with a specific perfume. Nina Ricci L'Air du Temps." He mumbles nonsensically. "A lovely scent. The odor sickens me. Grace and I were at Nordstrom a while back, and the same odor wafted through the entire floor. I didn't make it to the bathroom. Anticipatory emesis. Gracie thought I'd lost my mind."

Tick sits straight. "The notes. Where are they?"

Fox shivers again and flails his wrists, flapping his hands. "I wanted rid of them, y'know? Away from my family. Away from my little girl." He shakes his head. "Anyway, I kept them and ran them myself. They're from him, at least the ones with DNA. Peel-off stamps are a bane to forensics."

"What do the notes say?"

"Almost nothing. Numbers. No one ever made hide nor hair. Even I failed to understand them."

"Show me."

"Certainly." Fox waves his hand, shaking.

"You think this murderer, this rapist, is Conway? How sure are you?"

"Positive, with absolutely no admissible proof. No way to obtain a court-ordered DNA test." Fox focuses his gaze on the street between Le Metro and the Florida Atlantic University square, his face a study in mourning.

The partners settle into uneasy silence. Tick examines the grayed, deserted street between the restaurant and the FAU green. No students stroll on the lifeless campus. The human void always unsettles him. It's post-apocalyptic. A horror story based on the faded photo town flashes in Tick's mind.

"We can't bring the boy back. I think of death a lot. Too much." Fox leans forward and whispers. "Am I perverse to wonder whether death is easier than suffering? Of living? Death isn't the challenge, Tick. It's life. We know as well as anyone." He surrenders and grabs his phone.

He's diving for cover in his enchanted world, where the colors are bright, and he always wins.

"Life and this plodding game," Fox mutters. "We need fresh evidence, something to stick."

An SUV pulls into a slot on the side street, and a woman and three girls in sherbet dresses and strappy shoes jump out. Little pops of pink, yellow, and green invade Tick's black-and-white story. The little girls skip ahead of the woman, squealing and giggling. Streams of life flow from them, coloring the dull street. Anger fights with his ingrained sense of global responsibility.

I need to settle down. "Shay, man. We got something to go on here. We can stop this bastard dealing death out like playing cards."

"Death's not the challenge, Tick. It's life," Fox repeats. "You know as well as anyone." He speaks softly, his thumbs on his phone. "I'll give the letters to you. They're in my safe drawer at the station." The older man pulls a small silver key off his chain. "Theiss is coming over today. Think you can cover for a couple of hours? Plus, I have to visit an old friend."

"Sure, I'll work on those numbers. Kiss my sweetum for Uncle Tick. Man, she is sweet. Love her curly red hair." Thoughts of Theiss make life real again.

"I will."

Tick leans toward his partner over the table. "I'm going to push some extraordinary DNA on the pin. Meet you later? We will talk to the boy again, right?"

"Extraordinary DNA," Fox guffaws, cocking his head. "What's that? I'll have to sit you down and explain human biology to you."

"No, thanks." Tick picks up the bill and pushes the iron-scrolled chair back. "We headed to the hospital?"

"Well, there's a lucky bottle of port," the detective murmurs, playing with his phone.

The game's on. He's in control.

"Lucky?" Tick's expression is blank until Fox's words hit him. "Oh, lucky. Damnation, by all means. Get after your port, old man." His fury dissipates, and he's suddenly poured out. Exhausted, he throws a ten down on the tab. "Let's go. Sorry I took the keys. Gonna wear a mature guy out walking blocks in this sun when all these women are waiting. Must be fun."

"Grace told me to kiss you." Fox passes the younger man, who stops to give the money to a waiter.

"Shhh, you try kissin', and I'll deck you." Tick follows his partner down Main Street. "Old man's gotta buy a clue he ain't no stulla." *Fox has never heard 'stulla' before. He'll research the word when he gets home.*

fifteen
noon—the third day

JACOB MORENO IS PLANTING a small tree in the church garden when Fox pulls his car into a spot and strolls over. *A pretty purple flowering thing amid an explosion of colored plants. Gracie would like it.*

"Dr. Argall, how wonderful. We miss you," Jacob sticks his hand out and draws him in for a hug.

Fox stiffens, awkwardly patting the pastor's arm. "Reverend. Lovely tree. How's the garden growing?" He attempts levity, but the minister peers at him, concern etching his kind face.

"Growing masterfully, detective. And how's *your* garden growing?"

Taken aback by the question, Fox shifts his feet. "Growing." He points to the building. "Is Roof around?"

"He ran to get lunch for us and should be right back. Want to wait for him in the sanctuary?"

"Will do. Thanks." The detective tilts his head self-consciously and shoves his hands into his pockets before walking toward the Family Unity Church. Jacob's eyes burn into him as he works to stroll with nonchalance.

"The acoustic is by the stage," Jacob calls after him. "Check whether Roofie has tuned his guitar. He needs help from the perfect pitch the Lord dropped on you."

The Ruin of the Watcher

Fox turns in fatigued confusion, and the pastor winks.

"Oh, yes, Roof needs musical advice from me." *God, I'm tired.*

Wandering into the narthex and through the nave to the chancel, Fox scans the arched dome rising out of the crossing. Leaded glass windows glow and reflect dancing colors on the burnished oak benches. The soaring roof is extraordinary. *They don't make churches like this anymore. Well done, maestros. Bravo.*

An acoustic stands in the choir section of the red velvet-trimmed chancel. *Not the famous Lovely Yamaha. A darling Martin.* Fox can't recall having seen it before. He lifts the instrument from its stand. Warm, smooth wood slides under his fingers, balanced in weight.

When was the last time I played? Months, at least. Longer.

He sits on the front pew, pulls his long legs up, and cradles the guitar's body, strumming and checking the tuner. *Perfect. Of course.*

Fox holds the shining Martin with reverence, as he might hold Grace. His dad echoes in his ear, his accent heavy: 'A quality instrument is a thing to be cherished.'

'Who Am I?' flows from his hands on the unplugged acoustic. His baritone rises as if it's coming from someone else, his heart pounding in his chest.

Why have I stopped singing?

A shocking tenor fills the room. Fox doesn't turn as he closes his eyes to listen. *No other voice compares.*

Roofie is a musical genius who writes his own pieces. He can hear any song and hours later transcribe the music to paper, note for note. He plays and sings background for major Christian artists. *Roof always says when God saved him from the streets, he promised he would sing for Him alone. He keeps his promise with no regrets.*

For the last verse, Fox joins in a harmony familiar to both men, playing the ending chords on the sweet Martin for another two or three minutes. *It's a delight.*

Jacob waits at the rear of the domed apse, listening to the old friends. Roofie nods to his associate, and he slips out.

"Ellis 'the Fox' Argall, prodigy of prodigies, arrives to grace us with his presence. And his voice, his under-used gift from his God. Our Father and His angels weep when you clear the cobwebs, my errant friend." Roofie's words boom through the church.

"Edgar Allen 'Roofie' Parks, my oldest friend on this piece of land, this America. The closest man I have to a brother, with such lovely sentiment," Fox drawls. "Wonderful to know I'm never judged."

"Never judged, El, but would you have me lose my discernment?"

"No, never so, Roof." Fox grits his teeth as he focuses on the Spanish tile floor. *Hiding.*

'Roofie' is slang for Rohypnol, a benzodiazepine better known as the date rape drug. Roofie's mother conceived him during an assault. This nickname was the neighborhood boys' way of memorializing his sordid origins, so he would always remember who he was. The adolescent Roofie grasped the urban logic and embraced it; his mother never knew what the name meant. All the kids had nicknames, didn't they?

"What brings you here, El?"

"Does a man need a reason to visit his dearest friend?"

"I wish it wasn't so." Roofie stands his ground. "Want to worship or talk?"

"Talk," Fox mumbles. He flinches and forces himself to meet Roofie's gaze.

"Let's go, skedaddle. My ham and cheese is getting cold." He grins, slapping his friend on the arm as he strides away.

Fox sighs, trudging behind Roofie to his office, balling his fists in his trouser pockets.

sixteen
spring through christmas, 1983, ohio

THE OHIO STATE CAMPUS, Columbus, 1983

Ellis sits at a bar with his usual gang in the Short North, near the Ohio State campus. He watches Grace as he does most nights. It's fair to say he aggressively pursues her. Amused, she ignores him. She's always friendly, but their friends snicker and remind him she thinks 'he's prettier than any girl.'

"Do you think ESP will work?" Ben Fuller laughs as his friend obsesses. "Grace! Grace Dawes! Love me, not Ben!"

Ellis sits on the worn stool and leans against the bar's dark, now sticky wood. He has nothing edifying to say to Ben Fuller. His classmate has taken Grace out a few times, true.

Out out. Like alone.

Ben makes sure he's aware every time. Ellis dies slowly for hours, waiting for them to return and for Gracie to enter her own room alone.

"You two are delusional. Grace is not looking for a man. She loves neither of you nor will she."

Beth Wilson speaks from the end of the bar. Beth is Grace's best friend since they were on an academic quiz show in junior high. "We're here to work. Keep your eyes on the real prize, boys, an honors sash in our programs."

"Easy for you to say, Beth," Ben gripes. "I'm struggling for a B in PoliSci."

They turn as Grace heads toward them. "You guys ready? I've a test in the morning. Up early to study."

The friends leave the bar and decide to walk through Goodale Park, a faster route home. Ellis objects and is overruled. In the daylight hours, the park is a hangout for hooligans. At night, the danger grows, and the heavy trees provide a trap. Within minutes, several men approach the students.

"Well, lookee here, lookee here. We got some children out past their bedtime." A growling voice emerges from the darkness ahead of them. Eight men circle the friends as the speaker steps out from the shrubs.

Ben takes off through a hole in the throng and disappears.

The growling man laughs. "Watch the skinny one run."

For a few moments, the groups stand at an impasse.

"My friends!" Ellis projects his voice in a soothing lilt. He strolls out in front of the girls as if onstage, flinging his arms wide. "You have chosen the wrong 'children.' We spent our last dime in the bar yonder."

"Yeah, right," a man yells, and the rest guffaw.

Ellis waves in the bar's direction and deepens his accent. "I'm Ellis Cadnon Argall. I have both a black belt in taekwondo and a photographic memory. This leaves you two choices." He spins in a slow circle, and throwing a charming smile, he draws his pockets inside out. "Let me escort these ladies home, or—and I don't recommend this path for you, lads—try to take me on. This last choice will cause a terrible scene! Nothing we want on this fine night. Surely, a poor decision."

"You're crazy." Someone calls from the back of the gang.

Ellis laughs lightly. "Here's a proper idea! I could sing us a song. I also have a fabulous voice."

The monologue silences the men. Finally, one thug snorts, "How about 'Hey Jude,' asshole?"

A handsome, bulked-up man stands off the side of the group, silent.

This is their leader.

Ellis catches his eye and nods formally, bowing at the waist. "My best song, new friends! Be prepared."

After botching the first verse, he stops. "Well, that was ghastly. Just warming my voice!"

The leader says something rude under his breath, and the thugs chuckle.

Ellis grins at the man, not hiding his interest.

A few gang members advance toward Ellis and the girls until the leader puts his hands out and stops them. He laughs and begins the song with the voice of a tenor angel. The vocals shock them into rapt silence. Continuing to sing, the man turns around and motions for his crew to follow.

Ellis gestures to Beth and Grace to remain in the road as the gang disperses. "We head out of this park straight to home."

As they return to the girls' dorm, Ellis sings 'Hey Jude' in a lovely baritone. Beth laughs, punching him in the shoulder. Grace takes his arm, gazing into his face.

She sees me properly this time.

"Consider being the father of my children, El," Grace whispers, leaning against his shoulder.

No consideration necessary.

A few days later, Ellis visits the police station near his apartment and asks about the gang.

"Oh, no doubt. Roofie's gang." The desk sergeant glances from behind a scarred, raised counter and back at his paperwork. "Stay clear of them. Drugs, some fights. Been guns involved. A couple spent time in prison for drug running."

The officer eyes Ellis. "I mean what I say, kid. Stay away."

"Where does Roofie live?" Ellis asks. "Does he have a family?"

The sergeant reddens with irritation. "You listening? Stay. Away. The guy is not your friend or charity case."

"Oh, of course, I'm simply doing a university paper on such things. Thuggery in Central Ohio. Sociology class," Ellis grins, tilting his head and leaning into his accent.

"Good grief, kid. OK, listen, Roofie's mom is a wonderful woman, and the son—he's a man now." The police officer shakes his head. "She lives with her sister. They run a church on East Third Avenue."

"Thank you, sir."

"Sergeant." He's back to his paperwork. "Call me Sarge. Do something with your life, OK? Now, scat."

A young uniformed officer is standing on the front stairs as Ellis exits.

"Excuse me. How far is East Third Avenue from here?"

The cop glowers at him. "You a college kid?"

Ellis tosses the officer his most disarming smile. "Yes, I am."

"What do you want on East Third? Nothing for you on the east side. Where are you from? How long have you been in Columbus? You aren't familiar with the area."

"So sorry, let me introduce myself. I'm Ellis Argall. You're correct, of course. I'm from a tiny Welsh town in the UK. Hoping to meet a friend at church on East Third." He cocks his head to the side and smiles again.

The policeman sighs. "About five miles, give or take."

Five miles. "Well, I'm off then. Thank you, Officer. I'll be careful."

An hour later, he's still wandering. *At least I'm on the right street.* A voice calls out behind him.

"What in tarnation are you doin', child?"

Ellis turns to an elderly woman behind him, wearing a cotton house coat and leaning on a cane. "I'm not really lost," he grins. "This is the right place. I'm looking for Roofie's mum."

"Roofie's mom?" The woman frowns. "Now, boy, what do you want with her? How do you know Roofie?"

She squints her eyes, and her mouth narrows. "We don't need trouble here. You need to git."

"No, ma'am, I'm not looking for trouble. Or Roofie. No, ma'am. I'm looking for his mum." Ellis scrambles to fix what he's stepped in. "I met Roofie, I did, and not the best meeting, I'll admit. I was told his mum and aunt have a church, and I hoped I might sing with them."

The lady bursts into laughter. "Sing?" She assesses him carefully. "Sing. Well. We're worshippers, young man, not singers."

"Oh, I am, ma'am, certainly."

What does she mean? Still, she used the word 'we,' and he knew he was closer than in an hour and a half.

"OK, young man. I'll take you to Esther Parks. She'll decide if you come any further."

The two walk back in the opposite direction for about three blocks. They turn down an alley toward a small garage-type structure in the rear of a large house. A hanging sign in bright red letters declares, 'Our Home in Jesus Congregation Meets Here!'

The door stands open, and an older lady sings to herself, scrubbing a table with a bright pink sponge to her jaunty tune.

"What has the poor sponge ever done to you?" Ellis murmurs.

"Whoa, what?" The woman jumps at the voice and laughs. "Lost in love, child. Have you ever been lost in love?"

Putting people off their game is his ploy, and she has used the gambit against him. He tilts his head and grins.

"No matter, son, I know the One Who Loves as well as anyone I expect. I'll introduce you. Mattie, what have you brought us here?"

"He wants to 'sing,' Esther. He knows Roofie." Mattie's voice holds a warning, but her eyes are soft.

"Sing? Roofie?" Esther frowns for the briefest moment. "We don't sing, child. We worship. There's plenty a church that wants singers."

"No, ma'am. I want to worship." He grins again. "I may need some help."

Esther returns his smile. "Let's meet Mary. She's the senior pastor here and my sister." As an afterthought, she adds, "Roofie's mom."

―――

The determined Ellis returns repeatedly to the small church, making himself useful and forming a fast relationship with the two women.

On a Wednesday afternoon, weeks after they met, the sisters put Ellis in charge of cleaning the old garage for the nightly service. He's singing and washing the floor.

"What are you doing here?" A growl comes from the door.

Ellis glances to see Roofie. The man pushes his jacket aside to show a gun in his belt.

"Friend, your mum and auntie are right at the house." Ellis nods at Roofie's waist. "Want to reconsider?"

The man drops his jacket back. "I said, what are you doing here?"

"Learning to worship, son." Mary's sweet voice comes from behind the man. "Remember worship?"

Roofie blushes. His expression surges with rage, and he fights to remain silent.

"Edgar, come in. We're about to eat. Ellis's new favorite. Fried chicken with applesauce." Mary walks gently past her son into the congregational room, chatting. "Ellis's mom, his 'mum,' gave me the recipe for 'mash and leeks,' and I'm making it for Sunday dinner."

She moves to Ellis and stands beside him, looking evenly at Roofie. *A challenge.*

"We serve God here, dear one. We serve God and eat the best food. One or the other. Which one would you like?"

Roofie glares and retreats, disappearing down the alley. Mary puts her arm around Ellis and says, "I think Esther and I will walk you home today."

"No need. I'm not afraid of Roofie."

"You should be." Mary shrugs and wipes the table. "We will eat in a half hour. Will our floor be dry?"

"Yes, ma'am."

Roofie doesn't appear on the walk home or any day in the next few weeks. He visits his mother and aunt almost every day, careful to avoid Ellis. Christmas arrives before Roofie shows himself again.

Ellis sits in the congregational room, playing the Yamaha F335 acoustic guitar and singing.

"Ah," a voice snarls. "A miracle. My mom specializes in miracles. She'd tell you her God does. Your fresh voice a miracle from my mom's God, boy?"

Roofie looms in the door frame.

Ellis doesn't speak and changes the song to 'Even If.'

"Oh, he's funny too." Roofie moves inside the door and leans against the wall. "You never answered me. What are you doing here? I mean, here, at my mother's place. What are you playing at? I can tell you the game is a bad one for you."

"Roofie. Or should I call you Edgar? Your mother loved Edgar Allan Poe. She told me the story. Her first genuine experience with poetry."

The man seems to transport across the room, grasping Ellis by the neck. "You leave my mom and aunt alone. You stay away, or you will not live long enough to regret being an ass."

Far more intelligent than the rowdy boys and too beautiful for his own good, Ellis dealt with bullies his entire life. In fact, he hadn't met a single person in his tribe until he came to Ohio State. He holds Roofie's glare with a soft gaze without blinking.

He doesn't move to stop him. He rasps, "My father always said I attracted physical violence like a magnet attracts metal."

Roofie presses Ellis's throat until the younger man's eyes water. With a last squeeze, he lets go.

"Sorry. My comment was a bit off as I think back." Ellis bends his head from side to side with a grimace. "I wonder why you answer to 'Roofie.' Personally, I like the name Edgar. My uncle's middle name. One of them, anyway."

"Something's wrong with you. You leave my mother and aunt alone." Roofie balls his fists until his knuckles are white.

"Roofie. Edgar. Your mum says you're gifted. I marveled as you sang that night in Goodale Park. One of the most surprising performances, I'll admit. Esther calls you 'a genius.' Music by ear. I won't share our first meeting with your mum or aunt. Why don't you sit with me and worship just a bit?" Ellis's affect remains flat as finger marks darken on his throat.

"You're one odd dude. You are off," Roofie twists his mouth in a grimace.

"Yes, son, why don't you join Ellis and sing us a Christmas present?" Mary's voice comes from the door. "And if you don't keep this door closed, we'll freeze."

Panic flashes across Roofie's face. He makes for the door, but Esther is behind her sister and hugs him. "Your songs would be quite the present, Edgar."

Confusion twists the man's mouth, and he flushes.

Empathy floods Ellis. "Is this your Yamaha, Roofie? A peach."

"My grandfather's. Was my grandfather's." Roofie sputters, clearing his throat. "So freaking out of tune. Screeching."

"See, I couldn't hear a proper thing. Is it?" Ellis chuckles. "Ah, Edgar, set us straight here."

Roofie takes the guitar and fiddles with the tuner. A brief struggle plays in his eyes, then he sings 'Word of God Speak.'

After he finishes, silence fills the room, and Ellis understands the human reaction to Edgar Allen 'Roofie' Parks' voice.

Truly a marvel. A wide-ranging tenor with control to float into low notes and play there. I've never heard a purer voice in person in my life.

When Roofie starts a new song with a baritone part, Ellis joins in, watching him for a reaction. Roofie keeps singing, allowing him in.

I've won a minor victory. An opening. All I need.

Roofie sits in Ellis's dorm room in the early spring, discussing Grace. "Marry her, you idiot." He strums his Lovely Yamaha, shaking his head.

"I've a decade of school left, Roof. I can't marry every girl I want to bed."

This comment's too much for Roofie, who throws his head back, giggling in an un-bad-ass-thug way. "Yeah, why don't you start with all those other women in your line and come back to Gracie?"

Ellis frowns.

Roofie laughs until he cries at his own hilarity. "You can't talk to people. Hell, you can't meet eyes with people! Much less 'bed' anyone. You barely deserve Grace Dawes, you dog. Close the deal, or I may try my hand."

seventeen
lunch—the third day

FAMILY UNITY CHURCH, present day

"How can a brother in Christ help?" Roofie sits behind his banged-up wooden desk, which is covered with handwritten music, unwrapping his sandwich.

"I need another brain. I think my old nemesis from Boston has emerged in south Florida." The detective paces the small room.

"Conway?" Roofie pales. "Not the boys in the paper?"

Acid fills Fox's throat. "Afraid so."

"Sweet Jesus, let everything hidden come into the Light. Bring this man out, Lord. Let your man find him and stop him."

"I need help. I'm floundering."

"Those innocent boys. Oh, Lord. This is an opportunity now, El. You know this man. He's been haunting you for almost twenty years. He tracks you like you're prey. Take the demon out. The last boy died." Roofie shakes his head. "I'm acquainted with the latest child's extended family. The boy before him, the boy still in the hospital? His name is Deacon. He goes to Marion's church."

"No, I wasn't aware." Fox unravels these details. "Grace says he's doing much better than the first victim."

"He has challenging days, but loved ones surround him, and he knows his God," Roofie says. "Sit, El. Can you sit?"

"How do you explain this, Roof?" The words fall from Fox's mouth before he has time to regret them. "Where is God in this evil?"

Roofie is steady. "The world has fallen. You studied biological corruption. We fight the world, the flesh, and the enemy of our spirits. I remember one night in German Village, I sat with a young PhD student who explained a biologic phenomenon called apoptosis."

"Yes, programmed cell death. Every human is disintegrating." Fox says with a grim smile. "Why does He let pain and failure happen? Why?" He drops into a chair across from his friend and leans forward, his elbows on his knees to still his squirming.

"God made us first to love, as He loves us first. You can't love as He does without free will. God gave His free will to us. His greatest gift to us before His Son. 'In His image.' God created us to determine our choices, Ellis. We're made—called—to agree with Him and Him alone. When Adam agreed with God's enemy, death poured into mankind."

"Apoptosis."

Roofie lays his hand on Fox's hands, which are balled and tapping on the desktop. "As you explained, apoptosis is a biologic destruction timed into cells. We're spirits who have a soul and live in a physical body. We must choose to let our spirits lead. When we don't, the deteriorating physical body demands our full attention and dominates our free will, replacing God and becoming our idol. Money, sex, power—it doesn't matter. It's the same lie. Corruption. We make choices every day, and some choose extremes. You and I are painfully aware of man's failures."

"We are."

Roofie snorts and pushes himself from the desk. "Well, here I am preaching for free when I should require your attendance for the right to listen. Choose today whom you will serve—"

"As for me and my house, we will serve the Lord." Fox finishes the scripture.

"How is your house, my friend?" Roofie moves to Fox's side of the desk and sits on the edge, leaning toward his friend.

"Gracie is, as always, lovely perfection. She would want me to kiss you for her. No worries, I'll refrain." Fox glows as he mentions his wife. "Inexplicably, she continues to love me. Theiss is without measure. I can't explain her. She tries to sing! At less than a year old. She amazes me."

"I see Theiss every Wednesday and Sunday. She inherited her talent from her mommy and Uncle Roof," Roofie teases. "And Theiss's mommy? How is Marley, do you think?"

"Marley is with my granddaughter at practice every Wednesday and Sunday, yes?" Fox tilts his head, blinking his cat eyes. "You see her, too?"

"Yes, I do. I asked how *you* find her."

Fox twitches, his jaw tensing.

"When do you think you'll forgive Marley for taking Grace's time and attention? It's been almost three decades, Ellis. Will you let more time bleed from your relationship with your only child?"

Something in Fox wants to shut down, and his energy fades. *I can't fool Roofie.* "Well." He blinks again, dropping his head. "Well."

"Marley is beautiful and talented, the best of both her parents. El, here's the thing. She's an Ellis cut and paste; a female physical copy. Do you blame your clone for stealing your Gracie's attention?" Roofie rocks in the chair, staring at Fox. "Pray for release from bondage, brother. The foolishness is way below you. You're stealing from Marley. Stealing from Theiss, too. What pressure has your jealousy put on your beloved wife? Take fear straight on and kick it to the curb."

"Roof." The word is a whisper.

Roofie pats his hands on Fox's shoulders, embracing him. He

tightens his hold, feels his friend stiffen, and releases him. "I love you very much, my dear, dear friend. You're a wonder in my life, and I adore you. Hey, how about those Marlins? New stadium — when shall we make a date?"

Fox shuffles, fists clenched, tears streaming down his cheeks. "Tick wants to go to Opening Day." His voice breaks, and both men pretend they don't hear.

"Opening Day, we forget to worry for a few hours. Can't wait for a hot dog. They aren't the same anywhere else." Roofie puts his arm around his friend and walks him to the door. "Can we have you and Grace at church soon?"

"Maybe Sunday." Fox kisses Roofie on both cheeks, leaning his forehead against his friend's. Rare physical interaction usually reserved only for Grace.

"Just not this Sunday," Roofie mutters as the detective disappears.

Fox raises his hand to his friend, not looking back.

Not this Sunday.

eighteen
afternoon to evening—the third day

"MOMS!" Marley trills from the Argall's front door. "Nana!" She moves to Stewie's hysterical bit from Family Guy: "MOMM-MEEE. MOmmmee. MOM. MA. MOM. Mommeeee—"

"*What?*" Grace plays along, walking into the sunlit family room from the kitchen.

Her daughter is bouncing Theiss on her hip. "Hi." Marley grins with her father's mouth.

Does Fox grin? Really, openly grin? Grace can't remember.

"Say 'hi' to Nana, Theissey. Can you tell Nana 'hi'?" Marley is talking nonstop.

Fox calls Marley's chatter 'chundering.' *Vomiting.* Grace purses her lips, defensive for her daughter.

Theiss blinks slowly at her grandmother, her newest baby trick. Her delightful mother is on a roll, singing. Marley's always on a roll.

"She says 'hi' now, Moms, and 'hot,' and oh, so funny, she says 'TobyMac.' Well, 'Toe Ma!' She understands everything. She loves rap, anything with a hard beat. Loves jazz and blues. Oh, she loves blues. Theissey's going to be a musician. Her face lights! Uncle Roof says she's a miracle. She's a baby genius—" Marley's brain skips to another thought. "Baby Mozart!"

Marley spins and dances with her child, who gazes at her energetic mother with placid, blue eyes.

She is so like her father in every way—except for the extroverted energy, of course. Fox made a beautiful girl clone with Marley's dark, wavy hair and huge, pale green eyes. Her eyes are Fox's, yet they aren't. They're more subtle, more delicate.

She's even built like her dad. Almost 6 feet tall with broad shoulders. Made broader by the competitive swimming her Aunt Beth drove her to every morning from second grade through college. Next to Marley, I'm inconsequential. I'm shrinking.

Marley's chattering to Grace, to Theiss, to the open air. "Josh is in the car, waiting; his song was on. I gotta run, though. Is Aunt Beth coming? She said she might, she wanted to—she hasn't seen our baby for ages. Not for ages. They change so fast. I hate for anyone to miss this." She swings her little daughter around.

Her happiness flows out. My Marls spills happiness behind her, a sparkling trail of love.

Theiss reacts to her mother's glee, blinking and giggling, clapping her tiny hands. She wrinkles her little nose and screams again, her two white bottom teeth shining.

"What's all the shrieking?" Beth emerges at the family room door. "Who are those shrieking girlies? Where are my girls?"

"Aunt Beth! You're here!" Marley rushes to her beloved godmother. "She says 'hi' now, Aunt B, and 'hot,' and oh, just wait, she says 'TobyMac.' Well, 'Toe Ma!' Her face lights! She loves rap—"

Grace sighs with love for these women in her home. *They have the energy for themselves and a small, undeveloped country—it wouldn't be undeveloped long with these two. I can relax here. There is nothing to add; nothing's needed.*

Nothing demanded.

The two women leave Theiss with her and walk into the garden. Grace watches them, feeling like an outsider. *Beth and Marley are so alike—they could be mother and daughter.* She struggles with occasional jealous pangs, but Beth earned Marley.

She fought for my daughter when my weakness would have lost every battle.

Theiss pats her cheek. "Nah." The tiny voice is so gentle.

Grace looks into the child's innocent face and strokes her red curls. "My baby girl."

"Nah!" Theiss' dimple deepens, and her blue eyes twinkle.

"Yes, sweet, 'Nana.' Let's rearrange Nana's magnets on the fridge."

Later, when Marley leaves for the soccer game, Beth walks through the open French door. Grace is playing with Theiss on the floor.

"How are you?" The physician assesses her friend.

Beth constantly studies me. Grace shifts her hip in the chair, avoiding her friend's gaze. *She sees herself as my protector.*

When she found out she was pregnant with Marley, Beth suggested she become her obstetrician. Grace winced and laughed. *Who else would I want to deliver my baby?*

Autumn, 1984

The sun was going down, and darkness filled the claustrophobic living room in the Argalls' flat in Columbus. Grace sat hunched and crying. After denying the problems with Ellis for weeks, she finally broke down and called her best friend.

Beth snarled, punching the couch pillow. "He's an arrogant ass. He doesn't deserve you. And don't make excuses for him. I'm a 'genius,' too. Am I an ass?"

Grace squinted her eyes at her old friend. "Well."

The tension broke, and the two laughed until tears came.

"I'm delivering this baby, Gracie. She's mine, too," Beth

announced. "Wait and experience what an ass I can be if you deny me this!"

"You're like my sister. I will not flash my naughty bits when I'm sober."

"I prescribe drugs! I must deliver my godchild! You mean to tell me you'll let some strange quack bring my baby into the world? I'm serious. Who would you rather have in the room than me?"

"Ellis." Grace dropped her eyes.

Both women went silent. Beth to stop herself from saying what she wanted to say, and Grace to protect her husband. He would become her life's work.

Awkward moments passed before Beth patted Grace's bulging belly and reached for her hand. The affection flowed from Beth's hand to hers in a moment, and Grace decided. "OK, you win the chance to see my lady parts."

Beth leaned forward. "Y'know, they won't be my first."

Present Day

"Calling Grace Elisabeth Dawes." Beth drapes her tall frame across a chair with a smirk.

Grace pulls herself from her thoughts. "Gosh, yikes. Might be the Ambien, Beth. Marls thinks—"

"I'm aware of what 'Marls thinks.' She had me paged twenty-seven seconds after you two talked. Did I write an extended release? Where's the bottle?"

"In my pocketbook." Grace tries to remember where she left the little bag.

"You're keeping the sleeping pills in your purse? You plan on sleeping at work? In the car?" Beth shakes her head at her friend.

"No. I put them in my pocketbook."

"Because Ellis Argall doesn't mess with your *pocketbook*." Beth is tight-lipped.

"Don't start with me. Please."

Her friend flips her fingers into a 'W,' a childhood symbol they share. "Whatever."

Grace wants to talk about the unlucky lucky night, but she stops. *Shouldn't go there with Beth.* She spots her purse under the sofa. Theiss loves playing with her wallet. She reaches under the crushed velvet couch for the bag and takes out the pill bottle.

Beth glances at the label and says, "OK, no extended release. You can cut this in half. Marley's correct. The labeled dose is too high for most people."

Grace exhales. "How are people supposed to do the right thing if they aren't surrounded by physicians?"

"Hope they are surrounded by pharmacists." After decades, Beth's peculiar, dry sense of humor is still disconcerting. The physician chuckles and adds, "I hope they talk to their docs about any effects. Apart from an eight-hour sleep, I mean." Switching subjects, she says, "Ellis's hands are full with these assaults."

Irritation flashes through Grace, her cheeks heating. Beth's random subject flipping is a challenge. *I've surrounded myself with annoying, high-IQ people. Are the two innately connected?*

"Gracie? You're a bit floaty, girl. Cut the dose in half."

"Yes, the assault case is a bad, bad one. Long nights." Murder case. She doesn't point out the last child died. Nothing is public yet. She considers the unlucky night and again leaves her concern on the end of her tongue. Grace needs her loved ones close and loving one another. "Ready for dinner? Theiss will be ready soon for her napper."

"Food? Always." Beth rubs her hands together. "I'll make my arrabbiata. I brought everything."

"Of course you did." Grace smiles through a sigh. "What if my olive oil is less than appropriate? Or—gasp—my peppers aren't angry enough?"

"Your peppers are never angry enough, Gracie May," her friend says, hugging her. "I'm making leftovers for your husband,

and I want his tongue to scream, 'Beth cooked this meal!' You put my baby down for her nap."

Theiss is sound asleep, clutching refrigerator magnets in her chubby little fists.

The evening passes with wonderful food and the comfort only the oldest friends can bring. Beth's pager doesn't even buzz.

Fox hasn't come home when the kids come to collect Theiss. Beth leaves at the same time. Dusk is falling, and the sky is fading purple.

Grace stands at the door, trying to persuade them to stay longer. Her heart thumps in her throat. Fox will react if he misses his granddaughter.

"We can't wait." Marley gives an apologetic smile. "Class is at 8 a.m., and I gotta start my prep."

"Your dad would love to spend some time with Theiss. He'll be here soon." Grace wills them to come inside.

"Moms, in what parallel universe do we ever know when Dad is coming home?" Marley doesn't say this with any malice. She's a policeman's daughter. Raised in her dad's reality, she understands and accepts him.

Better than I do.

The three adults swing the baby between them as they leave. The giggles echo and fade in the darkness.

Grace sits in the new floral chaise she has put by the window, looking out at the darkening street. Her pulse quickens as Fox's headlights whip into the driveway. *He's driving too fast, rushing. He'll be so disappointed.* She clenches her fingernails into her palms as she waits for her husband to enter the back door.

"Where's Papa's guurrl?" Fox's accent is deep, slurring his words. Moving to Grace, he bends and kisses her head, noticing the couch. "What's this flowered thing?"

He's tired. Too tired. "Papa's girl had to leave, honey."

Her husband's handsome face drops. Grace doesn't miss the flash in his eyes.

"I guess Marley was busy."

The tension in his voice. Am I imagining things?

Fox throws his jacket off his shoulder and tries to shrug it on the chair in the hallway. He struggles with his left arm, flipping his hand violently until the coat comes off, inside out.

Wasn't imagining things.

He unbuckles his shoulder holster and squats to the gun safe below the table, fussing too long with the simple task.

Spring, 1990

Marley sat cross-legged on the floor beside her father as he performed his after-work ritual. She wasn't yet ten at the time. Every night, he took off his jacket, carefully unbuckled his shoulder holster and laid his holstered service weapon inside the safe under the heavy cherry table.

Grace saw the neutral, assessing expression on her daughter's small face as she asked her dad what he would do if a bad guy came in while they were sleeping upstairs. The pistol, she pointed out, was in the safe downstairs.

"Simple, girlie. I would throw him outta the window. The *ffenest, ventana,* as you prefer." Fox barely glanced at his daughter.

Marley concentrated on her dad with her pale eyes—his eyes—wheels turning. Finally, she said, "OK, Daddy. It's a very good plan."

Grace had to duck her chin to keep from laughing. Fox told Marley from an early age she 'needed a very good plan' whenever she ran to him with a problem. The day she wanted to have a tea party and didn't have enough chairs, when she needed to meet her friend Emily and didn't have a ride, or wanted an A in Writing and felt insecure.

"Do you have a good plan, girlie? All you need is a very good plan."

The day came when Fox found himself in a situation with a dangerous man. There was a break-in at a warehouse, and he was first to the scene and without a partner. He verbally warned as he entered the darkened silence. Halfway into the expanse of the warehouse, the burglar blocked his path to the door. Fox pulled every trick to get the man to surrender, talking the guy's head off when the criminal drew a gun and fired at him.

Fox returned fire and killed the guy, something he had avoided before that day.

Marley listened at the door as her parents discussed the shooting. She walked right up to her dad and asked if he had gone into the warehouse with a good plan. Grace sucked in her breath as Fox's eyes went stale.

After an eternity, he murmured, "I thought I had a very good plan, girl."

"Not every building has windows, Daddy," Marls whispered, kissing his cheek. "Which is why you have your gun."

After their young daughter scampered off, Fox sat in front of a baseball game on the TV for an hour, crying.

Present Day

"Grace?" Fox's voice hardens, dragging her back. "Hello? You here with me? Marley? Our daughter? Was she unable to sort her evening to stay and see her father?"

He's holding a brown folder, squeezing the cardboard so tight it has crumpled.

Faced with her sulking husband, Grace struggles to find the best thing to say. "Marley's class is early tomorrow, and she needs to prepare. Josh won his game."

"I'll play a game or two with Josh sometime." Fox drops his chin to his chest. "I used to have a mean kick." He shoves the scrunched folder into his backpack, bending the cardboard in two as he jams it in. He stomps into the kitchen, mumbling. "You ate dinner."

An accusation. You still have a mean kick, Ellis Argall.

Grace forces her voice to neutral, following her husband to the kitchen. He has his hands on the upper cabinet, tapping his forehead against the bottom edge of the door. "Beth came to visit Theiss and Marls. She made enough pasta for you. Want me to heat some dinner?" *His breathing is fast. Ragged.* "Lad. Want to talk?"

"Yes, and no, and maybe." Fox peeks at Grace from beneath his arms.

Unsure how to help, she teases. "You have a cute butt."

"Heard the rumor. Glad you like." He squeezes his hind end and wiggles but stays pressed against the cabinet.

"I have a lucky bottle." Desperation waves through her. *I'm fighting for neutral. Stay level.*

"Met with Roof for lunch today." His voice is a low rumble.

A subject change. OK. "Roof. Was the visit planned or spontaneous?"

"Spontaneous." Fox taps his head against the cabinet. "I'm not hungry."

The stimming always triggers an adrenaline rush in Grace. "Not hungry because of Roof or not hungry?"

Fox pulls himself from the cabinet and turns, leaning back on the counter, a red pressed mark on his forehead. "Want a movie?"

OK, we won't talk. "How about the baseball game? We have a late one."

"Bloody fantastic idea. In the bedroom." He jolts from the cabinets, breezing past his wife. He kisses her cheek as he passes her. "Make me fresh coffee, Gracie?"

The kitchen is her comfort place. Puttering, she washes the dishes, puts everything away, and makes coffee for Fox, taking the twenty minutes she needs to relax. Grace can't drink caffeine at night anymore. *Insomnia and heartburn. Fox is looking forward to the first espresso mini-IV human trials—a caffeine pump.*

She carries Fox's black coffee into the bedroom. His shirt and tie lie in a jumbled mess on the chair, and his shoes and trousers are piled on the floor right where he stepped out of them. He's asleep on top of the duvet. The TV isn't on.

Grace turns on the television, checks the baseball score, and heads into the bathroom. Fox never stirs. She stops and grabs the pill bottle from her purse. Forgetting she's supposed to split the tab, she swallows one without water.

nineteen
middle of the night —end of the third day

FOX FLIES AWAKE in the darkness, choking and unable to breathe, gulping. He throws himself from the bed. *Not enough air.* His heart pounding, he strides into the middle of the room, frantic.

Realization sets in as he recognizes his bedroom. *I can breathe.* His body relaxes. *I'm alive.* "Ah. Whew." He pants and slumps onto the bedside, hunched, his head in his hands.

Grace rolls toward him, pushing against his back. She's asleep, mumbling. Her hand searches for him, and she runs her fingers through the hair on his stomach. "What, darling, what—" Her voice trails off.

Fox studies his wife as she pushes against him. Grace can't wear clothes to bed anymore. Between hot flashes and creeping material, she lies awake all night. Worse, she tosses and sweats on them both.

My beautiful wife. He draws her in, naked and wrapped around him. Her hand drops to his lap as she falls into deeper sleep.

The familiar shiver rises. Staring at Grace asleep in the dark, he hesitates, then scoops her into his arms. "Gracie—" He pulls her to him, curled like a kitten. He presses his mouth to hers. "Gracie—"

"Lad—" Grace rouses and tries to return his attention.

He shoves his hand into the clutter inside his nightstand, looking for the pharma elixir bottle as he kisses his wife. The plastic container hits his fingers.

Grace struggles to respond to her husband. He moves more in desperation than passion. She simply can't stay awake.

His tears don't wait for a climax tonight. They flow down his face as his body demands the safety of his Gracie, his hiding place in her soul.

I'm alive.

twenty
early morning—the fourth day

FOX WANDERS out of the shower, a white towel wrapped around his hips. He rubs his dark, curly hair, and it flies in every direction. He hasn't shaved; a two-day stubble covers his cheeks.

"Well." Grace sits against the headboard. "I have a brush burn on my chin. Want to talk?"

"What?"

All big, innocent eyes. Blinking those lashes at me. She doesn't answer.

"Whaddaya mean?" His accent is heavy.

"Last night... or this morning? What time did you come in?"

"Dunno, Gracie. What's up?" He's messing with his phone.

"Ellis Argall." Grace crosses her arms. "I was ravished last night. Or this morning? Or in the middle of the night. I wasn't awake enough to be sure." She narrows her eyes.

"Ah. Must have been the pretend Ambien sex they talk about." Fox sits on his side of the bed, turned away from her, and dries between his toes. "Quite a side effect. How was it? Always wondered."

"I think Ambien sex is actual sex, while on Ambien, not imaginary sex you think you have." Grace grimaces as her husband pulls her into the ridiculous back and forth.

Fox tilts his head and raises his dark eyebrows, still focused on his feet. "Hmm. Was yours real or imaginary?" He strolls to the dresser, pulling out boxers, the wet towel dropping on the floor.

Swagger. He'd never stand around naked. "Feels real this morning."

"Hmm."

"Aren't you worried about being on display?" She hears herself taunting.

He doesn't answer. His back muscles flex as he steps into the boxers and sweeps on a white tee in a single motion. He fusses too long with his aftershave. The woodsy one Grace bought him for Christmas.

She watches him dress. *He's avoiding me. Afraid to meet my eyes.*

He stops fidgeting at his dresser and strides into the closet. "My brown trousers back? With the orangey tie, the one Marls gave me last birthday?"

"Salmon. It's salmon."

"Oh, well. *Sall*mon, then." A purposeful Welsh pronunciation separates him from his American wife. He sings under his breath, and she hears him pull his jacket from the hanger with a swish. A moment later, he walks out of the closet in a dark blue suit, flipping his light red tie to knot it. He smacks an air kiss at Grace from across the room without meeting her eyes. "Coffee at the department, pet. Love you."

twenty-one
morning—the fourth day

FOX TOSSES A RUMPLED, half-folded brown file onto his partner's desk, right on top of the report Tick is writing.

"Hey!" Tick yells. His partner disappears down the hall toward the coffee room.

"Read," he calls. "Ask if you have questions."

"Thanks, prick." *Fox Argall doesn't know when he's being an asshole.*

Tick flips open the folder, which contains medical reports. *Deacon. The boy on the fifth floor in the Jupiter Inlet Center.* The pathology examination describes the shiny spot under the boy's arm. *A computer chip. Like vets use to track dogs and cats. Only this one isn't traceable. This is simpler, with limited data.* He reads the information from the recovered chip, and his chest goes cold.

Fox's freaking address.

The name is Tice Argall. Tice? Who? He repeats 'Tice' in his head. *Damn. Damn. Theiss.* The icy rush in his rib cage turns to fire. *Her last name isn't Argall. The name doesn't seem to be the point.* The colonoscopy found another chip, buried in the child's intestines, with a different name: Grace Dawes. *Grace Dawes. Oh, Lord.*

A sickly sweet odor creeps from the file, from a fancy pink paper card in a forensic bag. The postmark is blank. *Blank? Can blank be a thing on mail?* Nothing on the note except numbers scrawled in several directions on the paper in dark rose-colored ink.

Tick isn't a praying man or hasn't been for a long time. He lowers his chin and whispers one. Then, he drags himself from his desk and goes to the coffee area.

Several deputies line the wall outside the break room. One jerks a thumb at the door. "Wouldn't go in if I was you, Tick." Another mumbles, "I'm sure as hell not."

His partner sits alone at the table in the center of the grayed linoleum. He's stretched out from the white folding chair, ankles crossed, hands tight under his arms. His face is thunder.

He's raging. "I'm so sorry, Fox, man. I mean, how you—how do I—"

The pale green eyes seem to glow, rimmed with bright red. He shrugs one shoulder.

Tick focuses on a spot on the floor, struggling for the words to help. He shakes himself. *I can't undo anything. Time to move on.* "OK, what's next? Cover Theiss, Marley, and Josh." He won't mention Grace. *I can't say her name aloud. Mentioning her would be a terrible thing to do on a day full of terrible things.*

The ice cube maker shrills, and Tick jumps. Fox's haunted eyes blink as he throws back an espresso.

"Have you—" Tick stops.

"No. I haven't told Grace. Ask Cap to cover my family." He crosses his arms on the table and drops his head.

"Oh, fuck, man. You haven't told Grace anything about this freaking shit? Damn, man. Shit."

"You need a new vocabulary." Fox grinds the statement out, voice muffled in his suit sleeves.

What are the right words?

Exhaling, Fox drags himself upright and pulls his phone out. Brick Breaker dings on. His face is blank.

I can't help. Tick slumps against the dingy beige wall. *I can't do a damn thing to help.* He heads back to the detective's area, glaring at the men in the hallway. As he passes them, he snarls, "You guys got any work, or am I the only one?"

Fifteen minutes later, his partner returns to his desk. Tick acknowledges him and keeps writing his daily. *Under-react.* "We're heading to the hospital, right?"

No answer.

"Shay? Hospital?"

Perfume wafts into the Detectives' Area. *Not the sweet stuff. A deep, spicy kind.* Tick looks up at a stunning woman staring at Fox. She has full, dark hair and wears sunglasses. *Man, that red dress.* She passes Tick and stops, smiling brightly at his partner, pushing her thigh against the edge of his desk. The red dress creeps up.

Damn.

I've seen her. The lady from the last death scene. The one I thought was media.

Fox ignores the woman, focusing on his phone.

Freakin' old man choosing his game right now? Tick's turbulent childhood leaves him incapable of suffering a silence or an awkward moment. "Hi! I'm Detective John Tickman."

The woman shoots Tick a dazzling smile, empty and dismissive, and returns to Fox. "Hello, El-lis." She draws his name out. "Winning?"

Ellis? He said he didn't recognize her at the scene. He was heading to run her off when I stopped him.

Fox speaks without raising his eyes from his phone, his voice light. "How can we help you?"

The woman stretches and sighs. Tick squirms and fights an urge to stand. *This is like a damn movie.*

She chuckles. "You were never very good at helping me."

Damn. Damn-nation.

Fox puts his phone down but doesn't look at her. "Natalie, what can I do for you?"

Fuck. Natalie.

She laughs again, throwing her head back. *Faking.* Tick can't pull his eyes from the diamond necklace circling her throat. *Does anything else sparkle like that?*

"Ah, Doc, what an opening. Points for resisting."

Doc?

Fox focuses on his phone, and the jaunty Brick Breaker tune plays. He's expressionless. "How's Boston? Still frigid, I imagine."

Boston.

Natalie pretends to think. "Hmm. Let me tell you a story. A small boy tries to make it safely home from church choir practice. He stops at the grocery to buy a soda. Suddenly, some predator grabs him. Next thing, he's in the Loxahatchee swamp, bleeding and barely able to walk." She stops and smiles at Fox, who ignores her.

"Ma'am," Tick begins.

"Imagine," she interrupts. "Snatched from a major grocer? How does this situation happen? Who permits these creatures to harm children? Who *failed*? Who allows those who prey on the innocent to remain?"

Nausea washes across Fox's face. He stands and staggers, steadying himself before vanishing down the corridor.

Leaving me with the strange woman. Natalie's beautiful eyes level at him, hard as the diamonds on her neck.

"Wow, ma'am. I'm sorry about what happened," Tick drawls in a thick country Florida accent. "Let me write down the details."

"Won't be necessary, Detective Hickman." Her eyes meet Tick's, but she isn't looking at him.

Tickman, he says to himself as she glides out of the exit. *She smiles, and nothing is inside.* He can't hurry to the break room fast enough. *No Fox.*

"Hey, man, seen Fox?" He asks the uniform at the coffee machine.

"Cap's office?" the deputy offers.

"Nah, thanks, man." *Where is he?* He remembers the nausea and heads for the bathroom, pushing the door open.

His partner leans against the sink, long legs crossed in front.

Smoke. He's smoking a fucking cigarette. A scene from The Rat Pack. I'm still in the damn movie.

"What the hell are you doing? Smoking?" He tries not to screech. *This is insane.* "Smoking in here is fu—freaking illegal!" The smoke alarm. The alarm dangles from the wall, wires torn loose.

"For— Shit, man, what's going on? Put the damn cigarette out. You're on video!" He flings his arm at the surveillance camera nestled in the bathroom ceiling.

Fox opens the tap and runs the cigarette under the stream. He tosses the wet tobacco in the trash, passing Tick to the door.

Fuck, fuck, fuck. Tick slides against the wall, panting.

An admin comes in, nose wrinkling at the odor. The man eyes the busted smoke alarm.

"What the hell are you lookin' at, kid?" Tick curls his hands into fists. He slams his knuckles into the tile wall to keep from swinging at the young man, who flinches and disappears.

Think, Tick. The report and the chips. His anger dissipates, replaced by panic and guilt pulsing through him. *The chips and that haughty woman. There's so much more to this. Still more.* He trudges to the detective's area, rolling his shoulders.

Fox sits at his desk, thumbs flipping on his device. "Ready for the hospital?"

So the chips, Natalie, and the bathroom didn't happen. OK, buddy. That's how we'll play. Tick unlocks his drawer and holsters his weapon. "Let's go, man."

As the partners wait for the security door to swish open, Tick glances at Cap's office. Their boss stands at the glass, watching them, his expression unreadable.

Fox pulls his phone from his pocket.

Brick Breaker. His personal protective force field.

They walk to the car and drive in silence.

Tension builds in Tick, and the anger returns. He squeezes his fingers into a fist and stretches them out, working to breathe in his abdomen. *Isolate and relax each muscle. Breathe.*

"Say what you need to say, Ticker."

"OK, I will. Who was the mystery lady, and what was she saying? Sounded like she was describing our first hit in this case."

Fox's thumbs fly over his phone. He doesn't respond.

Tick's shoulders tighten. His bruised hand aches, threatening. He counts his breaths to stay calm. *Roll each muscle, roll.*

After a long silence, Fox mumbles, "Meet Natalie Forester, Esquire, Boston, Mass, shark-at-law for hire, no hole too deep, no slime too slippery."

Makes sense. Tick swallows. "What was she saying?"

His partner whips around in his seat with such violence Tick flinches, jerking the car left of center. "Shit! Shit," he yells, fighting the automobile for control.

His partner's elegant face is twisted with venom. The menace is chilling on the obsessively controlled Fox.

Who the hell are you? Tick swerves to the side of the road, throwing the car in park. "What, man? What's going on here?"

His partner's chin is on his chest, focused on his game and shivering. His fingers grip the device as he struggles to regain his composure.

"Tighten each muscle, relax it, and roll down your body. Breathe."Tick's heart pounds. *Isolate each muscle, roll.*

Finally, Fox reaches out and puts his ring finger on Tick's thumping carotid artery.

"Remember this, John. If Natalie Forester tells you your own heart is beating, you need to question it."

twenty-two
late morning—the fourth day

THE DETECTIVES WALK in through the noisy hospital ER. Fox is so jacked up he's shaking.

Focus. He needs to focus. Tick aches for his partner. "What did you mean when you said you had 'skived it'? When you said the drugs had 'led you on'?"

"Skived, jumped past, missed the point. I assumed the drugs were so powerful— Well, the boys would have been de facto unconscious. The Demerol was a high dose. Allow the attacker to spirit the child away quickly, to chip their arm when they couldn't fight." Fox shuffles in his odd self-stimulation dance. "Still, confusing. Demerol isn't needed with the midazolam. Old-fashioned. Midazolam causes drowsiness, relieves anxiety, and, most importantly, in this case, prevents memories."

"Prevents memories?" Tick asks. "Like the IV I got at the dentist to remove my wisdom teeth?"

Fox nods. "Or when you have a colonoscopy. The drug inhibits the ability to create new memories during current events and doesn't impact longer-term memories." Pausing, his brows wrinkle in the effort. "I was left with why? Why take so much trouble? I assumed the kids were so drugged they wouldn't fight back, wouldn't remember. When I found the bloody cap, I realized I was wrong. I was wrong."

"Shay," Tick cautions. "Focus on the now."

"The second victim was alert enough to fight back, possibly because of the time to place the chip in the intestines combined with the rape. Or were they the same? This monster. He uses an implement to invade and inject the chip." He groans, grinding his fists into his eyes. "A chip with my personal information? To engage me, to taunt me? I struggle to understand such evil. Focusing on me."

"Shay."

"No, listen. Was leaving the message for me a mistake? Did the extra time allow his victim to come to some consciousness? Can we hope this child holds a memory of this sick twitch he doesn't quite remember?"

"If any victim can help, this one can. Deacon's sharp."

Fox shakes his head, berating himself. "I missed so much. Assumptions."

"Let me tell you something, bro." Tick stops and pokes Fox on the lapel. "The lawyer in you is talking, not the cop. Assumptions can lead you off for a time, yes. They also develop a great-cop gut. Your instincts are legend around here. We build scenarios and categories of events in our heads and best next steps. The way the evidence lays down. Part of being a fast-reacting cop. You do it better than anyone I've seen. Shake this off, Shay, so nothing slows us down."

Fox's eyes connect with his partner's and widen. A glint of recognition flashes.

Come back, man. Tick does a sarcastic 'say whaa?' head jiggle. "You aren't the only brains in the room, Welshman. We ready to visit this little guy? Want to call your wife and tell her we're here?"

"No." Fox flinches and puts his hand on the corridor's gray-green wall. He jerks it away like he's been burned and eyes his partner.

"Shay?"

A struggle flashes across the detective's face before he gathers himself. "No, Ticker. Grace has meetings on Wednesdays. No need to bother her."

"OK, man. Meetings. Right," Tick snorts. "Well, are you concerned about the family? Should we call Stella?"

They have permission to meet with the second boy, Deacon, whenever the child agrees.

"No."

Fox Argall gets access other people don't. Deacon's exceptional, too—articulate and calm in the horror. The kid wants to help. "We better call Stel. She'll hand you yo' ass, boy. I'm not sharing any blame. I'm tagging her."

"The perspective this artist used in this painting is so interesting. Almost alarming." Fox points at artwork hanging over the elevators.

He isn't worried about Stella. He doesn't worry much about people, period. "I'm calling Stel."

"Call, Ticker. There won't be a problem."

"I'll text her." He punches the elevator button. "Any fury and I'm absolutely pointing right at you, man."

The elevator dings its arrival, and Fox steps inside. "You won't have to."

"Someday, I'll ask what you did to her."

"Not today, I hope."

As the two men enter Deacon's bright room, an unfamiliar form faces the window.

Fox rushes past Tick into the room. "Marion, Marion, my sweetest."

An older lady swings to the entrance, and her face lights. She throws her arms to the detective. "Ellis Argall, you ornery mutt! Walk your pretty self over here."

"Marion." Fox squeezes her tight, lifting her off her feet.

He's touching her. Hugging her.

"Ellis, Ellis, Ellis. I won't ask how you've been. Jesus and I talk about you every day."

Tick wants to ask what Jesus has to say about a whole bunch of things. He holds his tongue.

Stel's firm voice startles them. "What does our Jesus have to say about 'im, Miss Marion?"

"Well, mostly alright. Let's remember what He says about us, sweet Stella Mae Weber Parks."

Marion grabs Fox's and Stel's hands and pulls them to the bed with Deacon and Tick. Somehow, she draws them into a secret circle. "He loves you, He loves you, He loves you. Anywhere we find excellence, He's calling you to remember Him."

Fox's mood flipped 180 degrees. It was a family gathering, a reunion. He was refreshed; the bitterness was gone.

"Marion Parks Clancy," Fox gestures to the young boy. "Let me introduce my friends. Deacon likes when we visit, don't you, Deac? Dear Marion, meet John Tickman, my partner in law enforcement. Miss Marion is Roof—Edgar's much prettier sister and, of course, your wonderful nurse Stella Mae's sister-in-law." He squirms, rare happiness flowing from him.

Caught in the upbeat energy, Tick stares at his provocative partner. *He's pushed the threats, the chips, Natalie, and the smelly letters into the shadows.* Only deep, bluish circles under the man's eyes are left from the morning's devastation.

"So nice to meet you, ma'am," Tick says.

Marion pulls the young sergeant into a hug. "My boy's partner is my boy, too."

Tick nods to Stel in jest, who frowns at him. "And lovely to see you, Miss Stella."

"You boys are a waste of my time. Do not tire my sweet Deacon, hear me?" Stella glares at Fox as she walks out, closing the door behind her. Stel is always glaring at Fox. Tick can't figure why.

The adults turn to Deacon. His small face is shining.

"Lovely, this family reunion, lad?" Fox smiles.

"Yes, sir."

"Yes, thoroughly likable, so what else?" The detective sits on the side of the bed. The Argall charm flows out like ribbons of caramel, weaving magic around the awe-struck boy. He purrs, his Welsh accent rolling. "Deacon, pet, how are you doing?"

The sound reminds Tick of a mother cat comforting her kittens.

"Could we talk? How should we? Alone, with Detective Tick, or what, *bachgen*?" [endearment, boy]

"We can talk, Detective Fox. Miss Marion knows it all, and Jesus tells her everything anyway!" Deacon chortles. A sudden pain flashes through his brown eyes, and his little face crumples.

Fox leans into Deacon's space, settling the child. He points to something tangled in the bedclothes and emphasizes his accent, exclaiming, "Deacon! What's this? A glove? A baseball glove?"

"Wow, the church. They got me this—a catcher's mitt, not just a baseball glove. It's brand new."

"New is something, right? Stiff, yeah? You'll have to work to sort it. Why is this catcher's glove different?"

Shot off like a cannon, Deacon explains specific differences in the mitts, gloves, and player positions. Fox lets him go on for five minutes about stitching and leather.

"Catchers direct the games. They're the leaders. They tell the pitcher what ball to pitch. Catchers motion the fielders to move where they should. Throw where they should." Deacon waves and points to an imaginary field, running his game.

"They're smart to capture every action," Fox agrees.

"More catchers are promoted to manager—more than any other position. They already manage as catchers, you know, they run the game." Slowing, his small face sags again. "Plus, they're not as tall, right? Pitchers are kinda tall these days."

The adults keep neutral faces. Deacon is not likely to make six feet.

"Detective Tick is a baseball maniac," Fox croons in his musical lilt. "A loosey goose for baseball, regular barmy."

Deacon giggles at the accent, which the Welshman is pushing hard.

"Aren't ya, Tick? Possible Deacon can call you 'Tick,' yeah?"

The boy's cheeks turn red. He side-eyes the six-foot-six-inch sergeant.

"He's a semi-giant, Deac. He can't help his size. He was born that way." Fox throws a conspiratorial glance at the tall man.

Tick leans against the hospital wall. "My buds call me 'Tick.' No one calls me 'Detective.' I sometimes forget I am one. Lots of people do." He glares at his partner.

"Hmm," Fox mumbles, rolling his eyes at the boy.

Deacon chuckles at the interplay.

"I shoulda been a baseball player," Tick continues. "My favorite player is Chooch Ruiz."

"RUUUizzz?" Deacon groans. "Oh, man, no dis, man, but Napoli, oh, man." The child's eyes are alight as he sets his argument.

A wicked grin spreads across Tick's face. "Never expected to find a Ranger fan in south Florida. Yup, Ruiz, he's a smart one."

"Ruiz is hitting this season, and that's a good thing, too—" the boy guffaws, shoving the mitt down on his fingers and waving his hand in the air. "The best stable in baseball, and the Phillies can't win! Napoli, all day long."

"OK, I'm done with you. A Ranger fan? What kind of Floridian are you? Chooch's got more guts than the Top Ten together." Tick growls in mock outrage.

"Can Deacon come to a game with us?" Fox interjects. "What do you say, Miss Marion? Are we going to cop it?"

"We might arrange a day out if Deacon does his schoolwork. I'll talk to his parents." Marion smiles, moving closer to the bed. "Did you want to discuss the case?"

Deacon draws a quick breath and turns to the window.

"Well, I have a question or two. We need a smart set of eyes for our mystery, Deacon. Someone who gives the complete picture. The entire field." Fox taps the glove with his finger, catching the child's eyes. "Ready, mate? Stay here with me."

"Ready." Deacon swallows hard and sits straight.

"What's Rule Number One?" Fox asks.

The boy locks eyes with the detective. "Feels like everything people do is about you. The truth is, what people do is almost always about *them*."

"Why is this Rule Number One?"

"Because to work the entire field, we must learn to stop seeing everything through our own eyes. We have to use the facts and not our feelings. Our feelings can be used as lies, and we miss the truth. The truth is what we want and what we need."

"Cracking." Fox pulls his tape recorder out of his jacket pocket. "Understand why I record our conversations?" He repeats this each time they talk.

"To protect us. So we remember what we said."

"Bingo." Fox clicks on the recorder. Deacon, this is Lieutenant Argall. Would it be OK if I taped us today?"

"Yes, sir."

"Can you remember for me about the very beginning, where you were when everything started?"

The struggle on his boyish face is heartbreaking as he works hard to answer the questions, trying to remember everything. Much is lost forever, and the child grieves at his inability to offer the details. The adults thank God for the memory loss.

Deacon quivers and sits straight again, flipping his IV line away. "I was walking out of the school. A guy, I think... I thought he was a guy. He grabbed me from behind and smacked me. I felt a funny pinching. I think now he stuck me with a needle. Afterward, my head was real spinny. He wore old ladies' gloves. They were mostly white, I guess. Not white, yellow, and pinky in places."

Old blood, Tick muses. *The bastard uses the same gloves each time and washes them. A ritual.*

"OK, now," Fox urges. "Do you remember going into the brush?"

Deacon's eyes squeeze shut. "No, not really, I woke up, kinda not awake, and my arm—" The boy unconsciously reaches under his arm, where Stel had shown Fox the shiny spot. "And my elbow, man, my arm hurt."

He breaks my heart. An IV left a hematoma. Such a deep bruise. Badly inserted. Missed the vein. From the struggle? Or is this guy an amateur with IV drugs? And why not an oral liquid like the other child? Would he need the IV if he wanted them unconscious for longer to insert the chip? The last child had no IV. No intestinal chip, just the arm.

"You woke in the brush?" Fox gently prompts the youngster, interrupting Tick's thoughts.

"Yes, well, I guess, I was—I really hurt, and—" Deacon sighs and closes his eyes, drawing his arms across his chest. "Lots of blood."

"Rule Number One, Deacon. This isn't your fault." Fox smiles, reassuring the child. "Here's what I'm wondering. Do you remember hitting anyone?"

Deacon's pupils dilate. His face changes and Tick can't read him.

The boy turns to the window, the adults following his gaze. The room fades as the moment fills with loud chirping from an oriole couple perched outside. A chattering flock of unruly starlings swoops and swings.

Tick inhales. *Life goes on in the middle of our pain.*

When Deacon faces the detective, his eyes are determined. "I remember. I remember seeing his face. He had makeup on, but kinda like a clown, kinda smeared. I clobbered him right in the face. I gave him an uppercut."

Fox presses his lips together in a grim smile. "Might you have hurt him?" He points to the boy's left hand.

Confusion flashes on the young face. After a moment, Deacon stretches his arm to Fox, rubbing his knuckles. An abrasion covers the top of his hand, with bruising across his center fingers.

"Yes, I did. I'm strong for my size. I put my legs into the punch, and I clobbered the guy."

Energy sparks in the room.

"Catchers always have sturdy legs," Tick agrees, meeting his partner's eyes.

Deacon beams at Tick. "They have to, right?" His eyes register exhaustion as he works to interact with the detectives.

"Right." Tick smiles back at the kid's courage. Hot tears fly into his eyes, and he chokes, fighting hatred for the scumbag who hurt this baby.

"Now I remember I musta passed out again. I may have gotten him." Deacon's mouth twitches as he looks at Fox, his face alight for approval. "Then he hit me, and I think I passed out again."

"Caught you on the chin?" Fox murmurs, encouraging the boy.

Deacon rubs his jaw, where a bruise is turning green and yellow. "I think I got him, Detective Fox. I kinda woke up once and here's this face in front of me, this snakey smile, and he only had one front tooth."

An adrenaline rush washes through Tick. His eyes meet Fox's again.

We have him.

twenty-three
noon—the fourth day

THE PARTNERS STAND like twelve-year-olds in the glassed office in front of Cap, who is steaming. Sweat forms on their boss' nose. Tick can't stop staring at the glistening beads.

"Know what I'm looking at?" Cap slams both fists on his desk, making his computer keyboard jump and slide sideways. "*Maaates?*"

Cap punches his fist at the desktop screen, tilting it backward. His face is bluish. The senior officer launches from his chair and storms around the desk, stopping an inch from the partners. He unclenches his shaking hands and jabs his finger into Tick's solar plexus. "Any thoughts, Sergeant Tickman? No?"

Damnation.

Cap swings to Fox, who is swiping at his shoes. "Doctor Argall? No? Nothing from our favorite smart-ass? I have an idea. You two assholes call your mommies to come and explain—" he hisses, leaning into their faces, "—what happened in my fucking bathroom."

"Well, Cap," Fox starts.

Cap turns on him. "Shut up. Shut up. You shut your mouth." He jams his finger in Fox's tie, punctuating each word.

The normally cocky detective is wide-eyed, stammering.

Tick snickers nervously, his heart rate soaring. He's never seen Fox so—so what? His Gran would say 'discombobulated.'

"Wanker," Tick mouths to his partner. He heard Fox call a fellow officer the epithet under his breath when the guy took his personal coffee mug. *Just the best word. If I were ten, I'd say the word over and over. Wanker, wanker. Fits so many places.*

"What's funny?" Spittle flies on Tick's face as Cap shoves a finger back into his chest. "You think you skive? You do not."

He's changing colors, turning red, then white, like he's beginning the fission process, splitting molecules in the air. *What's 'skive' mean?*

"Cap," Fox whispers.

My partner has balls. I'll give him props. Man.

Cap whirls on his lieutenant. "I said shut the fuck up. I'm finding this very... distasteful. You... Counselor," he sneers, stabbing his finger in Fox's tie again, leaning a millimeter from his nose. "You broke a slew of local, state, and federal laws, *Counselor*, and I'm willing to bet my mortgage this was a fucking hissy fit. Oh, yes, we're smarter than everyone else, so the rules are different. The rules. Are. Not. *Fucking. Different.*"

Yikes.

"Get out. Leave my sight, both of you." The furious captain spins and knocks a jade plant off his desk. The moist soil sprays across Cap's pristine floor, leaving green bits everywhere.

Like a broken, miniature Christmas tree.

Apoplectic, Cap yells, "No. I'm leaving, and you two are cleaning this shit. I'm warning you, run the fuck out of my sight and stay out. Don't make a mistake with me here." He storms out, reaches back, and grabs his door with both hands, slamming the thick metal edge as hard as possible. The entire floor rattles.

Not one person outside in the detective area raises their head. The two men stand stock still for a full minute.

"Crikey." Fox takes his handkerchief from his jacket pocket and rubs his cheek.

Tick yanks the cotton square from Fox and wipes his own

face. An invisible bubble bursts, tension flowing from him like a silky river. Giddy, he prances past his partner. "Well, *Counselor*, you're cleaning this shit. Meet you in the car, and you better go out the east side exit. Use the freaking vacuum, asshole."

"Wanker." Fox huffs at Tick's back.

"Want the sweeper?" Missy leans in the door as Tick is leaving.

"Miss, sweet girl—"

"This is me seeing right through you, Dr. Charm Pants. Not a single chance I clean this for you. I already did your only favor. I explained to the entire team I'd seriously hurt anyone taking pictures or videotaping. I protect my own, *pet*."

"Innocence is dead. I mourn for the cynicism of the younger generation."

"This way, Detective." Missy's arm sweeps Fox out the door. "The closet, north wall, first door on the right. Here's a house-keeping tip—scoop the dirt pile and loose leaves into the trash first. Otherwise, the dust will blow out the back onto your lovely suit."

Twenty-five minutes later, Fox opens the car door. Tick's head is thrown back on his headrest, and he's singing loudly to 'Set Fire To The Rain.'

"You're off-key. It's not bad. I might train you." Fox examines his hands, connects his seat belt, and cleans his fingernails.

Tick slowly raises his middle finger. "Need a manicure, girly-man? Don't drop your mess in my car."

Fox continues cleaning. "I think they call this 'potting dirt.' Naff." His phone chimes, and his mouth twists as he reads the text.

"What, man?" Tick leans to read the message, but the sun glares onto the screen. "I can't read it."

"The phone call I got yesterday. Wasn't a burner."

"Fantastic! What did tech find?"
"The number belongs to a woman. Lydia Conway."
Tick whistles. "Conway?"
"Lydia Conway. Providence, Rhode Island."
"Is that the freakin' ex-wife?" Tick's mouth drops open.
"Nah. The daughter." *What can this mean?* Fox sighs, feeling the acid creep into his throat.

twenty-four
late afternoon—the fourth day

"I'M NOT GOING to Rhode Island." Fox rests against Cap's door, burying himself in Brick Breaker.

Shay, man, what are you doing? Tick watches the two men. *Cap just put you in your place. He's gonna blow.*

"Fox." Cap leans across the desk to bully his lead detective but loses the energy, falling back in his chair.

Cap's giving in to him. The text from Lydia Conway changes everything.

"You wouldn't go to Rhode Island either." Fox's voice is barely audible. "You wouldn't leave town if a whack job was threatening your family."

"Who? Who better?" The senior officer sighs.

"I'm not sure I'd ever be the right person," Fox says, glued to his game. "Lydia blames me. She hates me, detests me. I got her father off on the charges her mother made. I stole her chance for rescue. He's loose because of me, no doubt continuing to hurt her. Why would she talk to me?"

The men are silent. Cap heads to his orchid display.

Everyone has a hiding place. "Why don't I make the Rhode Island trip?" Tick asks.

Fox doesn't respond, thumbs flicking the ball across his screen.

The captain is suddenly focused on measuring water for his orchids.

"Is anyone going to tell me the rest?" Tick sighs. *I don't have the fight to be pissed anymore.*

His partner keeps his eyes on his phone, his mouth tight. His thumbs aren't moving.

Cap takes a deep breath, grinding his teeth. He turns his head sideways to stretch his neck.

"Fuck." Tick flings his hands up in frustration.

"Stop, Ticker, stop." Fox groans. "Stop, for everything holy. I'm telling you, you sound like an absolute moron with that mouth." Moving to the window, the detective presses his forehead against the cool glass. Condensation forms around his breath.

"Cap? People, please talk to me." Tick pinches the bridge of his nose, rubbing his eyes. *This is exhausting.*

The captain exhales. "OK. Fox, this is my call, not yours. Tick goes to Providence. Time to trust your partners. Ticker, here's the rest. The bastard's a United States senator."

"A U.S. senator?" Tick stammers. "No, he was a state politician decades ago. With the legal trouble? Are we talking about the same guy?"

Cap nods. "Conway. He's currently a sitting U.S. senator from Massachusetts."

A soft, sickening moan comes from Fox. He sounds like a dying animal. "Gracie will never forgive me. Oh, God. I've lost my darling girl—" His voice is muffled as he presses against the glass.

"Shay, where is your head on this? How are you connected to this guy? This senator?" *What's this anguish? Grace? So fucking much more to this mess.*

Cap shakes his head. "You listen to me, boy. Everything you could do, you did. You told everyone. You gave depositions. You testified, quit your damn job, changed your entire life. Put everything at risk."

A low howl comes from Fox as he taps his head on the glass.

"You took your family and moved down the country," Cap

implores. "Left everything behind. Mac did everything possible; he gave the last great measure. Are you saying Mac failed? Neglected you and me? Failed those children?"

Mac? This name is new.

Fox doesn't respond and bangs his head harder. *He's gonna break the glass.* Streaks run down the steamed pane.

"The bastard would have buried you, boy. Do you understand me? Buried you." Cap presses. "You had a wife, a child. What were you supposed to do? Mac and I marveled at you; this nerdy floof. Your courage—fucking stubbornness."

An eerie 'squee' sound repeats in the heavy room as Fox rolls his forehead against the glass. The pink and purple sunset shines off the window, and his tear-stained cheeks appear bruised. When he speaks, it's a whisper. "I should have shot him when I had the chance. I had the chance."

He staggers into the corner by the window, his hands covering his face. "I knew this. Everything. My job was to blow his bloody head off his bloody body."

It takes more than espresso before the detective can continue. The Blanton's bourbon comes out of Cap's locked filing cabinet. The senior officer pours a double shot of the honey-colored drink, and Fox drains the glass in one gulp.

"Explain, Shay. Talk to me," Tick begs.

"The court ordered and sealed the DNA evidence for the divorce," Fox whispers, pressed into the corner. He keeps stopping for lengths of time to brush non-existent lint from his trousers.

Over and over.

Tick's struggle not to scream grows in his chest as he waits impatiently. *Roll, breathe.*

"So many misses. If Conway hadn't finagled those tests?" Fox continues. "He was clean with those specific kids. Oh, my God." He slides down the wall.

"Breathe, Shay."

"The tests, he *wanted* those tests ordered. He asked Tom Masters for me."

Tick sits on the floor a few feet away. "Explain it to me. What about the tests?"

"He wanted me, a physician, a researcher, to order those tests. Ellis Argall, a renowned expert on molecular genetics, physician, and lawyer, said the tests were necessary! He even used Gracie—A PhD bioethicist from Harvard—as a reference in his request for the subpoenas. He set me as a part of his scheme. As a state senator, he used me and pressured the judge to obtain the subpoenas. I'm certain the testing wouldn't have been ordered without my gravitas. Shady at the time, and I was so stupid! So deep in the dark."

"Dammit, forget that shit." Cap growls and slams a broken container into his trashcan. It splinters, and shards fly across the floor. "You were a lawyer, not a fucking mind reader. No one could have known any of it. Mac knew you took a copy of the bastard's lab report?"

"No." Fox pants, his cheeks wet, and he struggles for calm. "We had the kids. We thought we had the kids to testify. What benefit to drag Mac into my wrongdoing? Risk the administrative assistant who gave the file to me?"

The detective twists his shoulders, trying to relieve the pain. "In the end, none of the children willing to prosecute had Conway's DNA. No one willing to testify had his particular infections. We always figured he paid the right ones off."

Fox lurches from the corner and begins pacing behind Cap's desk. He stops and sits hard in the leather chair, pounding the surface with both fists. "Conway became careful after his divorce. After I taught him how to be careful."

Laying his head on his arms, he finishes the story, his words muffled and despairing. "I couldn't continue to put Grace and Marley at risk. We had to leave. Leave. I had done enough harm campaigning for my redemption." He spits the last sentence out, bitter.

Man. These guys can keep a secret. "Can you guys tell me about this Mac? Who is he?"

Cap sighs, and Fox flinches so hard he slips on the leather chair.

"You start, Skip," the detective mutters. "You loved him first and longer."

Skip?

"I began my career in Boston." The captain stifles a cough. "My police career."

"What?" Tick sparks surprise.

"I'm from New York, hence no funky Boston accent." Cap nods to Fox, who does his raised brow-blink thing. "I was on my first streets with Mac. He'd been a sergeant and got knocked back—some scuffle with the Bigs. Mac wasn't much into politics."

Fox doesn't quite manage a smile. "Angus 'Mac' Macraith, a Scot from the Highlands. He always trilled."

Cap laughs, sending light into the desolate room. The smothering pain lifts.

A sweet, low chuckle comes from Fox. "Mac had a gorgeous and cheeky Welsh wife who forced him to learn the language. Macraith was the one who called me 'Fox.' My middle name is Cadnon. Cadno is Welsh for 'fox.' He thought the whole thing hilarious. He was *coegni, goeglyd,* sarcastic. Thought I was a twit. 'A foppish fool.' *'Byddwch yn gorffen mewn ffolineb, bachgen.'* You'll end in folly, boy. He would shake his head at me with such drama!"

Fox and Cap laugh together in the memories.

So surreal. So much hidden with these two.

Standing, Fox shudders as he remembers. "He always said *'Bydd yn rhaid i mi ateb i'ch mam yn eich angladd.'"* Translating the Welsh, he continues. "'I'm going to have to answer to your mother at your funeral.' Mac put on a horrible Welsh accent. He butchered our poetic language."

Cap nods in recollection. "Yeah, Mac walked into my office one day and said, 'Why, you'll never believe, Skipper, me boy.

Found me a real one, 'e's pure teckle, a braw bairn or a bampot, I dinnae ken."

A thick brogue. This is crazy.

Cap laughs. "Ever wonder about my sad-ass nickname? People called 'Skip' have even worse real names. My Màthair, God rest her soul, was pure Scots to her toes, and she named me Farquar— 'Dearest One' in Gaelic. My dad is Welsh." Cap glares at the men. He won't allow any trouble to come from this name tidbit.

Fox lifts his hands in a flutter of 'Hey, nothing here.'

Tick squirms in his seat like an excited child.

"Anyway," Cap continues, "Mac said your partner was either the best rookie he'd ever had or the worst, depending on the day. Macraith started calling him 'Fox' to get his goat. Well, turned out, right? He meant the nickname as a compliment sometimes, too."

Fox is back to Brick Breaker, his fingers shaking.

"OK, enough old home shit. *Cael go iawn, bachgen. Gennym waith i'w wneud.*" [Get real, boy. We have work to do.] "So Mac didn't find out you had copies of the DNA lab reports?"

Fox moans softly, eyes locked on his game.

"Well, I want them."

The detective's jaw tightens. He puts his phone on the table and balls his fists, fully engaging Cap for the first time. *"Ni allaf fentro pawb rwy'n eu caru. Allwch chi ddim deall?"* [I can't risk everyone I love. Can't you understand?]

"Hey! I'm back in a frickin' movie, only now I need subtitles." Tick stands between Fox and Cap, unsure who to address. "English, people. A little left out here."

"No, dammit," Cap storms to his lieutenant, crowding him. "I want your evidence. You're going to trust me on this one. I'm not a fool, Dr. Argall, regardless of your opinions."

Fox cringes, opening his mouth to speak.

"No." Cap pushes further into his detective's personal space. "No, listen. We gotta flush this bastard out. We got him. I'm done hiding. We're done hiding. You've decided he beat you in Massachusetts. I'm sure you think he did. We have him this time. We got the DNA on these Florida kids. He left a mess here. He's decided he doesn't need to be careful anymore. We have pathogenic DNA."

"Skipper."

"No, we've got him. We need his specimen—a legally acquired specimen we can use in court. I'm gonna fix this. Find real information. I didn't have the juice back then. I'm ready now. I'll pull every string I've collected for the last twenty years. No one will be quick to step on a U.S. senator, but my chits are in place."

"Right." Fox groans again, crumpling back in the chair. His misery flows into the room.

This is like the kid's game, The Floor Is Lava. Fox is spewing red pain everywhere. Cap's physical management—domination—of his partner amazes him. *How did I miss this? How did I miss their relationship?*

The captain crouches in front of his detective and talks softly. "If I can find what I want, I promise I'll never show anyone the divorce papers. You've kept this report for a reason, *fy ffrind*. [my friend] Most lawyers would have destroyed the documents long ago. Think. *Ymddiried yn fab i mi.* [Trust me, son.] Let me make a few calls."

twenty-five
evening—the fourth day

ROOFIE PARKS SITS in the Argall's kitchen with his best friend, working hard to encourage him. "The first day I saw you in the Short North of Columbus, you strolled out in front of Grace and Beth, facing down some of the nastiest dudes I ever ran with. We were mostly high, and we were all carrying. You acted like you were on Broadway delivering a stage monologue. The only reason I spoke to you again was that whack turn you did—the one spin. What struck me? You purposely turned your back on us, showing us we couldn't lay a hand on you. Faith. You shoved your faith in our faces. Your faith was the Spirit of the Lord, and you shook me. You helped change my life. You changed my life."

"He uses donkeys to speak, remember?" Fox mumbles, trying to smile. "You only talked to me again 'cause yo Momma Mary woulda kicked yo ass. Plus, you loved my singing." Fox's urbanese is horrific. His eyes are on his phone, but he hasn't picked it off the table.

The itching of countless addicts.

Roof slips the phone into his pocket. "If Momma was here right now, it'd be your Welsh ass she'd kick. Time to stop hiding. Way past time to deal with this mess. Force the darkness into the light. Don't let shame take your power away. We're about to speak to your wife, and you're going to tell her everything. Everything. Dearest El. Let your God help you."

Fox shivers and slumps in the chair. "I wish Momma was here. She loved me best."

"I wish she was here, too. What do you think she'd say? 'I ain't there, and God is. He'll never leave you or forsake you, even unto the ends of the earth.' El. This must end here. This can't stand between you and Gracie anymore. I can't help you block your wife out any longer. Truth is, I should never have agreed to keep this secret in the first place. I don't think we can do this alone. I don't think we have a good enough plan."

"We don't have a good enough plan."

"So. Let's go. Our wives are in the bedroom."

When the men walk into the darkened master, Grace sits on their four-poster bed, leaning into Stel. Stel's face shows her clear desperation to break the 'do not murder' law, starting with Fox.

"Grace. *Stel.*" Roof speaks harshly. "We must talk to you both."

"Talk?" Grace raises her hands to cover her eyes. *No, no.*

"This case, the sexual assaults. The divorce Ellis was dragged into? When he quit his job at the firm. The husband they defended was a pedophile. We believe this is the same man. Now, he's a murderer." Roofie takes Grace's small hand in his.

"But... What?" Grace jerks. "Murder? A pedophile? In Boston... The guy didn't, right? Fox got the court orders for the tests, and Tom Masters proved the husband didn't abuse the children. They won the divorce case. The wife went away. She went away."

Roof's words drag Grace backward. She's falling into an old nightmare buried for years. The numbness seeps in. "You left because of the politics in the office, right? Right? You left because Tom forced you into a case you didn't believe in. You thought Tom helped that man bully his wife."

The room darkens as the sun moves behind a cloud. Fox sits on Grace's makeup stool, his broad back slumped. He pulls at his trousers below the knee, smoothing the legs over and over.

"Yes," Roof steps in. "In the case with the little girls in Massachusetts, Conway was not guilty of the specific assaults. He wasn't innocent of other atrocities. Ellis discovered the truth and took the info to Tom. But the law firm wasn't helpful. In the end, he couldn't stop anything, not legally."

Pulling Grace into his arms, Roofie lays his head on hers. "El went after them. Conway is a powerful man. He was a state senator. Now, he's a U.S. senator. Your husband is an endless thorn in his side." Roof stops to let the words take hold.

No, this can't be true. "No, nothing like that happened." Grace pulls from Roofie and collapses into Stel's arms, who sits like a stone.

Stel's staring at Fox. She would set fire to him with her eyes if she could.

"Lad? Where's Tick? Does he know all this? Cap? Does Cap know?" Grace grasps for her husband, a ghost in the room—a specter threatening to fade away.

The sunlight washes back into the room, covering Fox. He's rocking on the stool, which clicks under his weight.

Click, click.

"Fresh evidence came up," Roofie continues, "and Tick is going to meet Conway's daughter. He flew to Rhode Island to interview her. He's due to land in—" Roof checks his watch. "Twenty-five minutes. We need to understand—and accept—that this is about to blow open. Did you hear me? Conway is now a United States senator. What will happen is still a mystery, but we must be together."

Roof puts his arm around his wife and catches her eye. "We are family," he reminds her.

Tears flow down Fox's face, his sobs echoing in the room. "The divorce DNA. My failure. My guilt, allowing this monster to stay in life, to keep hurting children. I ran instead of throwing myself in front of those babies. I took my own and ran," he whispers.

"U.S. senator? What is this?" Grace faces her husband, her voice rising. "You kept this from me? When we came here, we were running? From what? Has Marley... Theiss? Have they been in danger all this time?"

Click. Click. Fox rocks, his hand flipping in his lap and turning an imaginary phone. His palpable pain fills the room.

He's mine to protect.

Grace turns to Roofie and Stella. "Can you leave us alone for a while?"

"Why have you kept this from me?" Grace moves to the makeup table and sinks to the floor, laying her forehead on her husband's knees. "How have you had this pain, and I've never known? How, my wonderful love, my perfect Ladislaw? Why suffer without letting me in? Without trusting me?"

Minutes pass as Fox continues to rock. Grace climbs on his lap and takes his face in her hands, leaning into him until their noses touch. She rubs her dry cheek on his wet one. She kisses his eyes and mouth, pressing her head into his chest. Finally, he pulls her into his arms.

"Nothing, my Lad, nothing can shake our love," Grace murmurs. "Have you forgotten the song you sang to me at our wedding? 'We are stitched together.'"

He cries into her neck, soaking her collar. "Mac and I, we tried everything, Gracie. We lost. We lost. Mac died, and I ran."

"Tell me what happened." She pulls her husband's chin to her and forces him to meet her eyes. "Tell me the complete story."

He pulls away from her, moaning. "Everything started at

Marley's seventh birthday party." He hesitates and inhales a deep breath. "I'm going to tell you. I'll say everything out loud. Give me a minute."

twenty-six
the mac story

FOX BURIES his head in his wife's neck. "Conway likes young boys." *I'm not lying, am I?* The guilt hits him. "It's me he's after, Gracie. I'm not sure what form this might take."

Grace pulls her husband's face to her. "Look at me. He was after you when Mac died?"

He tries to pull away, but she holds him tight. "No. You must stay focused with me here and face me. Tell me the story. I deserve your trust."

I can't say some things out loud. Some words won't come out. "I confronted Masters with some evidence I found. Masters refused to act. We rowed. I quit my job the same day. You remember the day." Fox moans and starts to rock.

"Stay with me, Lad. We are one. One."

"I worked with Mac. We pushed. We kept pushing. We got nowhere. Conway was protected on every side. Powerful protection. Mostly in panic, I went for my PhD in criminology. I needed to understand how to fight him. I went to the Police Academy in Boston. *Roeddwn i'n dwp, nid wyf in ddoeth.* [I was stupid, I'm not wise.] Instead of making the problem disappear, becoming a cop made everything worse with Conway, like bursting an infection open. So much more to this man's malevolence. So much more. Every place I went, Conway appeared. He seemed... Obsessed. Each day, we found another nest of Conway's snakes."

"And you confronted him? Fought him?"

I hid. I hid until I was unable to find another hole. "I'm not proud. I didn't see any way to win. I tried to avoid him. I understood what he was. Maybe I was the only one with actual information willing to admit what he was. In the end, I understood the futility. I didn't want the fight. Mac did. He forced me to face Conway, to try to... I dunno," he groans. "Gracie, I was a gnat, and he was the eagle."

"How was Mac involved?"

"Mac walked in behind me one day as I read a note Conway sent me." Fox pales. *I'm sliding down into an abyss.*

"A note? Conway sent you a note?"

"Yes, but unsigned, and I was guessing."

"How did you guess? Lad, talk out loud. I can tell you're struggling and burying the lede. Say everything."

"OK. The notes referred to the children—the children from his divorce case. A number of little girls, you'll remember. Conway's daughter. She was Marley's age. Seven at the time. Also, a couple of boys. The children were found to have sexually transmitted diseases. The year of the divorce case, Mac was a captain in the Boston Precinct Five — Back Bay and Beacon Hill. The girls were all from the neighborhood. He was pulled in after I raised the trouble at the law firm. I met Mac before I quit the firm. I told him about the situation. Mac pushed as much as possible, more than was good for his career. Kept trying to tie Conway to the cases. I quit the firm. While in grad school, during my criminology doctorate? Before I went to the Academy, I was helping Mac and Skip Harley. Skip was Mac's sergeant at the time." Fox drops his eyes, unable to meet Grace's gaze.

"Skip." Grace's tone is calm and neutral. "You knew Cap in Boston."

"Yes."

"OK, keep going." Grace tightens her hug.

"Most of the kids were tested. I helped with the molecular typing. We had trouble getting Conway's DNA. We couldn't obtain a blood sample. We needed a few samples, really. The negotiations went back and forth. His attorneys said he'd give samples, then they'd claim he had already given them, but poof. I raised every point, kept pestering. Nothing. Suddenly, a man showed at the precinct and voluntarily gave samples. We connected the little girls to him. The little boys? They went poof, like Conway's 'voluntary samples.' Gone. Parents wouldn't talk. We were convinced Conway had paid them off, but..."

"So, the man?"

"He was convicted. He got twenty years."

"But the case wasn't over."

"No. Mac kept getting reports of assaults on little boys." Fox squirms and puts Grace on the floor. He turns on the stool, spinning.

Click, click.

"I'll give you a minute, Lad, but this is not enough. Tell me the rest."

"I got notes."

"Notes. What did the notes say?"

"They described where the next assault was going to happen."

"And the assaults occurred as the notes described." Grace inhales.

"Yes. Working for Macraith at the station, I kept hearing rumors and getting notes. Young boys. Harmed, damaged young boys kept appearing like mice on a doorstep. We stopped some assaults, but others... Mac was incensed. He kept going to Conway's offices. Interviewing his staff. Mac wouldn't let me near. He said I was 'the bastard's obsession,' his goal, and he wasn't giving me to Conway as a prize. We could find nothing. Nothing. He was so clean." Fox spun back and forth, twisting on the stool in a rhythm.

Click, click.

"Finally, Mac's bosses stepped in. Conway had complained.

Would have been bad enough if the crimes ended there. But the notes to me and the assaults kept up. We chased them all down. Every few weeks, distressed parents would appear at the station. Each time, a note was left with the child. The parents' notes were mostly nonsense, but Mac and I knew. We understood the connection."

Fox stands and roars in pain, shaking his fists in the air. His voice cracks, tears covering his pale face. "Eventually, a note came in Welsh. I held Mac off for the first ones, but the Welsh note sent him storming up the chain, not being careful. When he met resistance... I should say apathy, a wall of apathy. Mac blew his famous Scots stack. They put him on suspension for insubordination. He threatened a press conference. He threatened to release the notes. To send them to independent forensics."

Tears pour down Fox's cheeks, soaking his collar and tie. His rocking and spinning become a violent shaking. "Too much, too much. I'm going down. I need my phone, Gracie. Roofie has my phone."

"I'll get your phone, honey. Stay here."

Grace retrieves the phone, and Fox begins playing Brick Breaker, hunched over, standing up.

Watching her husband, Grace forces even breaths, waiting, giving him time. She wraps her arms around his waist from behind. She holds him tight and sways. Minutes pass.

As he settles, she murmurs, "Can you finish for me?"

Fox's voice has gone flat. "Mac went to the media, which forced the Prosecuting Attorney to start an investigation. Conway's team sent their own false media reports to Boston PD HQ. Threatened to release slander. The false information claimed Mac ran a pedophile ring and accused the senator because Conway wouldn't protect him. I was terrified for him, Grace. I saw the end. It was all too clear. The chess match was ending. The Black Queen, Conway's Queen, was closing in. Mac was cornered, no moves left. He didn't see. He refused to accept we lost." Fox taps his head on the poster at the end of the bed, sobbing uncontrollably.

Grace turns her husband toward her, pulling him into her arms. "Hold me, Lad. Dance with me. Sing with me." She begins singing 'Able.' She draws her husband into her dance and sings to him until he calms.

"I sat outside Mac's house for two weeks until Mac caught me," Fox whispers. "He blasted me. Attacked me. He actually smacked me in the jaw. Told me he'd either kick my ass or take a beating from me, no matter. He forced me to leave."

Fox breaks down again. "He told me to leave. A showdown was coming. He still thought he could win. The board, Gracie, we were checkmated. Conway had us cornered. The first night I didn't stay, they found Mac in his back alley, his old army gun in his mouth."

Anger flickers in Grace's eyes. "Gun? Not a heart attack."

"The decisions about the cover-up were over my head, Gracie. They said the lie was for Mac's wife. For insurance. I believed the goal was to stop any investigation. Conway was... is obsessed with me. Mac and me, and Skip. We made so many enemies on the way. They murdered Mac in that alley, Gracie. Murdered."

"What happened? After Mac?"

"The notes and attacks stopped after Mac's murder, but Conway held a press conference and publicly blamed Mac and me, said we were incompetent in an old, completely separate investigation. A man used to intimidating and winning. Conway's team released false evidence. Reported Mac framed Conway. The false reports got the investigation dropped. I had to extricate you and Marley, so I brought you here. This evil man hates me, Grace. Me, alive... simply breathing scratches his craw bloody. Puts you and Marley, Theiss. Puts everyone in danger."

"Is this senator threatening you now?" Grace asks. "Has he threatened our daughter? Theiss?"

Fox buries his face in Grace's neck again, repeating, "He likes young boys."

I can't tell her about the chips. About the letters. The guilt hits him again, and he doubles over, panting. "He wants me, Gracie. We have men at Marley's already. Now, after this. This mess. We'll bring Marley and Josh up to speed and station officers here."

Roofie puts his head in the bedroom door. "A deputy here, El. He's been sent to bring you to your captain."

Hanging head in his hands, Fox says, "We have some leads, Grace... Roof. I don't have any idea when I'll be back. Could be awhile."

"Stel and I will be here with Grace."

"You'll have a couple of strapping lads as well." Fox pulls himself up. For the first time, he feels every day of his fifty years. "I need a shower."

As Fox leaves the bedroom for the bath, Roof comes in and hugs Grace. The need to stay strong disappeared out of the door with her husband, and she finally cries. "Roof. How did it happen? Mac's murder was a bomb in our lives. And now I find the answers were lies. How did my husband go through this without telling me?"

"How many times does Ellis share his work?" Roofie sighs. "His life. They had killed Mac. You were in school, and you had a small child. He thought keeping the truth from you and leaving was the best way to protect you and Marley. After all this time, he thought he did the right thing. Try to put the questions aside, Grace, just for a while. We'll face this together. Let's pray to Jesus He opens the darkness and spews this creature out into the light, so he can be found."

Stel leans against the bedroom door. "Be found? He's sitting in the Capitol Building." She speaks in acid tones. Where is he? There is no secret. Where is he? He's in the District of Columbia, running the country."

Roof turns to his wife. "Stel, love, he wasn't in the Capitol or DC when he raped the last little boys. He was in south Florida."

Grace moans. "If this predator is after Fox, none of us are safe. Where's Marley? Where's Theiss?"

"The police are at their house," Roof says. "We need to trust Ellis."

"Trust Ellis," Stel mutters. "There's always that."

twenty-seven
morning—the fifth day

YAWNING, Tick stretches his arms in the open air outside the Palm Beach Sheriff's Office. "Lydia Conway had a lot to say. She kept saying, 'This detective doctor is in the middle.' She believes you're connected physically and in this bizarre metaphysical way. Connected to her family. Especially to her father. She doesn't call him 'father.' She doesn't call him anything. Weird. You work hard to track with her." Tick fights back another yawn.

"Breathe, John, your yawning is stress. You yawn because you fail to breathe properly." Fox strolls with his hands in his pockets, kicking at nothing and looking down, his chin on his chest. "So, Lydia is still challenged."

Tick notes the now-familiar guilt in his partner's voice. "She's convinced these recent assaults are her father, but she has no evidence. I'm not sure Lydia's a legal testifier. She's jacked."

"So, we've gotten on his radar again, with no benefit." Fox sounds defeated. He closes his eyes and drops back.

Tick turns, creating a barrier with his arm. "Man, are you laboring under the extremely bogus delusion you're not already on this guy's radar?"

His partner stares blankly at him.

Fox face number six. The 'I need a minute to absorb the fact you may have a point' face.

The older man shoves his hands in his pockets for his phone. "No. No, of course not. Sorry, mate. You're right."

They continue the walk in silence. Tick builds the confidence to ask the question squirming in his mind since the diamond lady came into the station.

"Wanna tell me about this Natalie chick?"

"No." Fox quickens his pace.

"Is she going to be in our grills with the first boy?" Tick runs in front and blocks his partner again.

"Yes." The glare. A flash of anger before Fox pulls his eyes down.

Tick pauses. "She's from Boston. How can she be here, anyway? Don't attorneys have areas where they practice?"

Fox sighs, gazing at the sky. "You're not gonna drop this? Yes, and no. Attorneys can practice any place they can pass the bar. Any state. They can also practice federal law, Supreme Court."

"So, she's OK to practice here?"

"Maybe. Might be aligned with a local attorney." Fox whips to face his partner. "Jigger, Ticker! Bingo!"

He turns on his polished heel and heads back in the opposite direction. "Come on. I'll drive."

Tick hesitates, looking at his suddenly upbeat partner's coattails.

He's almost skipping. What the hell just happened? He runs after his partner to their car.

Sitting uncomfortably in the unfamiliar passenger seat, Tick turns on the radio, looking for a rap station.

Fox slaps his hand. "I drive, I pick."

"OK, dawg."

His partner flips until he finds "This is Your Life," humming along as Jon Foreman plays the lead-in chords. In the second refrain, Fox sings over him and taps his hands on the steering wheel. The song finishes as he turns into Jupiter Hospital and pulls into a space by the ER.

"Man, exactly who are you? You're a truly odd guy." Tick shakes his head.

Fox chuckles.

Triumph. This is precisely the reaction he wanted.

"I'm a man with close to five decades of life and lots of surprises for young whippets who think they know me."

"Amen, word."

"Yes, *word.*" Fox snickers again, and Tick realizes laughter has been scarce.

"We seein' Grace? Deacon?"

Fox shakes involuntarily, frowning. "Best not meet Grace for this one. Not sure she's here today. I should do this alone, but frankly, I need a witness. Even my partner."

"I'm here." *Not sure where Grace is? Right.*

They stride into the ER, and Tick waves to Dalia, a nurse who is standing by the open doors to the emergency department.

"Need buzzing in, detectives?" When Dalia smiles, her face lights.

Tick puts his fingers to his lips. "Shhh." He smiles back. "Yeah, D, hook us up?"

As the partners walk down the hall to the elevators, Fox murmurs, "When are you going to ask the lovely woman out?"

Tick shoves him into the wall.

"Should we have called?" Tick wonders out loud as they approach the administrative department.

"No. No warning for this one. Surprise is our friend."

They arrive at the administrative floor. Fox turns away from Grace's office, and Tick follows him down the hall. At the other end, his partner stops at a door. Tick's pulse quickens at the nameplate. *Ben Fuller.* Fox doesn't knock. He opens the door and walks in.

The attorney is sitting at his desk. He hesitates as the men walk in, and forces his frown into a smile. "Ellis. And Tick, if I remember correctly? I would ask 'to what do I owe this pleasure,' but having known you so long, I'm going to go out on a limb and say this will not be a cheerful conversation." He slides his chair out and stands in front of his desk to face the detectives.

He hopes the conversation won't be happy. Ben Fuller is itching for a fight with Fox and it stinks all over him.

"When did you meet Natalie Forester?" Fox tosses the question out like a gauntlet.

"Natalie... Forester." Ben scrambles enough for the detectives to note. He decides not to lie. "Natalie and I met at a National Healthcare Lawyers meeting."

Smart call not to lie. Tick can feel Fox simmering. *I wonder how well this Ben understands Fox?*

"You remember? What a conference. Remember Baltimore? Crab cakes were something. Why do you ask?" Ben rattles.

He's working too hard. Knows enough to be afraid.

"Why would you be a party to a lawsuit with the first assault victim?" Fox cross-examines Ben, leaning into his space.

"I would hardly describe our proprietary discussions as me, or the hospital, being 'a party' to anything. Or have you forgotten how 'party' is defined, in legal terms, I mean? First year of law school? 'Any person involved in a transaction or proceeding'? The hospital is not involved in any such actions."

"I'm fairly certain Leonard Forash and Nancy Bittren wouldn't worry about the formal definition of the term. As heads of the Board here, they might have some concerns if they were aware you consider your conversations with a potential litigant's counsel *proprietary*. Conversations you have never mentioned to them. Or the transfer of protected health information to a third party. To a potential litigant's counsel? *Proprietary.*" Fox's voice is light, but he's coiled tight, like a snake ready to strike. "Proprietary to the hospital or to you?"

Ben pales.

Tick remembers the way his face whitened the last time they met. *This guy is a wuss.*

"Well, Ben," Fox says. "Speak."

The lawyer is greenish with red splotches growing on his cheeks.

"If you aren't..." the detective growls, showing his teeth. "...*perceptive* enough to notice what's in front of your nose? I'm afraid you may be stepping in it."

The danger in the room rises, and Tick's blood pressure rises in response. His partner doesn't blow often, but when he does, Tick can't always stop him. Last time, Tick joked Fox was like Mr. Hyde.

"I'm aware you and Natalie have some sort of history." Ben tries to sound brave, but dark, wet spots grow under the arms of his expensive arctic-blue shirt. The attorney flashes panic.

You fucking wanker. Tick holds his breath, tensing. Ready to jump if anyone makes a move. *Shit, man.*

Fox stands so still, time has stopped. Ben pants in shortened breaths. Loud seconds click away on his wall clock.

"Ben, I'm so sorry for your pain. No one in the world would ever understand what you lost better than I do." His partner speaks in a low, controlled voice. His face fills with compassion — or something close. "Grace is the other half of me, and I think thirty years have proven the truth. I could no more have walked away from my wife than tear my own leg off. Please, please don't risk yourself for something in the past. Over for decades. Stop fighting a fight over long ago."

Ben's face goes whiter.

How is that possible?

Leaning nose to nose with the lawyer, Fox almost whispers. "You cannot call Forester off. You're out of your league with her. But, I beg you. Pull yourself away from this cliff before Natalie Forester pushes you off." Stepping back, he gives Ben a minute to respond before turning and walking out.

Tick nods at Ben and follows his partner out the door. Fox's back disappears into the stairwell. He runs to the top of the stairs as the detective is turning down the next flight.

"You're never going to tell me about Natalie, are you?"
"Nope."

twenty-eight
noon—the fifth day

"OK, PEOPLE." Cap calls for silence in the patrol room. Tick and Fox squash into the line of detectives who stand against the wall.

"Listen. We've moved forward in the sexual assault cases, which we believe involve a single perpetrator. We've tentatively identified the suspect, but we're not ready to release the information yet. As we have experienced before, the detectives assigned to the case and their families have received threats."

An ominous rumble threads through the group. Their eyes avoid Fox and Tick, but the ranks close around them.

Cap waves his hands. "Enough. This is our job. We're all grown-up boys and girls. We do this for a living, right? Anyone like to leave? Ring the bell? Now's the time."

Murmurs flow from the crowd.

"Lieutenant Argall received a letter, and I want you to see and smell the note because we believe the suspect may have this odor. Not unknown for hinkies to show here at the station, right? The letter says nothing. Just simple numbers that appear random. Note, forensics hasn't finished. No touching. This meeting is to let you know we're taking the threats seriously and to bring you as up-to-date as early as we can. We're done here. To work! Folks depend on us to be on."

Cap motions for the partners to follow him into his office. The men go in, and Tick shuts the door.

"Nothing in Rhode Island. No matter. I got something." Cap says. He's reading his paperwork. "I got the prick's DNA."

A strangled noise bursts from Fox.

The senior officer winces but continues. "I won't be discussing this 'get' in any detail until you two are taking shots at my wake, so don't ask. This is mine, for Mac. Forensics, our forensics, is running right now. I figure we have about eleven minutes before the Fibbies cluster in our corners, hanging like bats from our ceilings. Fact is, they can't stop us at this point. I won't let them. I'll release this information in whatever way I need to bring him down. This is over, hear me, Lieutenant? It's over. No one in this room needs the report. Am I right? Right."

The detective is at his window perch, tapping his forehead on the blinds.

The static in the room is too much for Tick, who can't keep his eyes off his anguished partner. "What's next, Cap?" he asks.

"We wait."

twenty-nine
late night—the fifth day

MARLEY AND JOSH'S house sits in darkness. The crickets chirp from the bushes bordering the tiny cottage. The street lamps are those dim ones, kind of orange and flickering. Between the crickets, the refrigerator whirling, and his earphones, the young officer never hears the screen door at the back of the house crack open.

The feet shuffle inside and stop, waiting for the police officer in the hallway to move.

He doesn't.

A figure creeps behind the officer and tightens a wet rag over his face. The officer tries to turn into the heavy form behind him, but his body slumps forward. The intruder pulls his silenced weapon out, then stops and drops the 9mm back into his holster. He takes a second to evaluate his surroundings.

The highchair sits against the wall next to the tiny table, with a pink bib reading 'I am loved' lying on the tray. He listens for any sound. Hearing none, he silently inches toward the stairs.

He knocked out the officer outside, but the risk of a silenced gunshot is more than he wants to venture — unless he has no choice. He enters the hall and removes his 9mm, moves by each door, listening. Steady breathing in one room. In another, the rustling and tiny sigh of a baby. He stops for a full minute. He opens the door to the baby's room and slips inside.

A white crib waits in the darkness. The intruder holsters his weapon, stops, and listens. Only the sweet gurgle of the sleeping child. As he steps forward, a shadow darts in front of him and smashes the gunman's nose with a solid 'thwump,' dropping him like a stone.

Fox flips on the light. No baby lies in the crib, just a recorder. The detective squats, takes the gun, and cuffs the motionless man. He picks up his walkie and taps Tick downstairs. "Everything OK?"

"I almost had to take him out. I thought he was going to kill Ethan." Tick's voice is tight.

So far, so good. Fox sighs. The man is bleeding on his granddaughter's floor. He wants to kick him. He knows he'll never force the image from his mind. Finally, he turns and sticks his head out Theiss' door, calling for the two officers in the next room. "To the infirmary and to holding ASAP. I want him ready to talk within the hour."

"Yes sir, Lieutenant Argall, yes." The young men look down at the crumpled man with the crushed nose.

"You hit down, with all your strength, against the bridge of the nose. Use your elbow or the flat of your hand. Elbow's best, if you've got the angle. You'd be strong to do this with your hand, but there you have it. Down, understand? You hit upward and you'll drive the nasal bone into the brain tissue. Naff with your file," Fox instructs. "I'm joking. An old wives' tale. You can't actually kill someone that way. Not easily anyway."

The young officers stare back.

Fox waves his hand to the door. "Off, off. Be off."

The officers lift the unconscious man and scurry away. The man has bled quite a bit on a fluffy pink rose rug.

Marley might be mad.

Downstairs, Tick stands over Ethan, who is now sitting. The young man chokes in nausea.

"Be glad you put those earphones in," Fox says. "They kept you from getting shot. My buddy, here, he's an ex-Ranger sharpshooter with a dead eye. But maybe he would've missed?"

Ethan looks uncertainly at the big sergeant, who makes a rude gesture to his partner behind his back.

"If I miss at ten feet, someone oughta put me out of my sore-ass misery," Tick scoffs.

Tilting his head to the side, Fox's mouth is a thin line. "You'll have a significant headache, deputy. Nothing will help the pain except remembering you didn't die today. Go home, drink as much water as you can, even as you chunder. We'll write the absence slip and submit for you with your sergeant. But here you go, pet. I want you to reconsider *ever* using noise-canceling earphones on the job in future. Today, they helped you. Every other day, your job is to be aware of everything happening. *Pen ffwl. Gyda fi?* With me? Good."

Ethan shakes his head, dazed.

"Chunder is Brit for puking, bro, and I think the Lieutenant called you a dickhead," Tick says. "And you can be sure the twitch wouldn't have his gun outta the holster before lights out."

"I would never call you such a thing, Ethan. I'd call you a silly head." Fox mutters 'wanker' in Tick's ear as he brushes past, on his way to the back door.

Tick follows his partner outside. "Who is this thug? Just an iceman?"

"Don't suspect so." Fox opens the car door and gets in. "I think this whole thing is something Conway would hold quite close to his chest. Can't see an independent hired gun. Seems too risky."

"Yeah, makes more sense if he's someone close to Conway. Close, but a throwaway. Like any of this sh — stuff makes sense." Tick is stupidly pleased he didn't curse, high on adrenaline. He grins at his partner.

"Everyone is a throwaway with Conway." Fox grimaces. "If

you not cursing every two minutes is all I can get today, John, I'm blessed. Take me to holding. I want at this guy."

Fox calls Roofie from the car and updates him on the situation. "A bruised elbow, nothing more. Tell..." He stops. "Roof, kiss Gracie for me, will you?" He wants to beg his friend to fix everything, to restore what the locusts have eaten by the time he gets home. Instead, he clicks off.

"Grace and Marley OK? I wasn't gonna tell you, but you look like you've come off a three-day bender."

Fox sighs. "I dunno. Even if the entire ordeal were over, I'm knackered. I've lost the plot." He's slurring his words, accent heavy.

"I think I want a molto-choco-latte-isco. Want something?" Tick swings into a twenty-four-hour coffee shop.

"That's not a proper drink. I think it's a line from *Lady Marmalade*." Fox smiles. His phone is in his hand, playing his game.

"Lady who? Is she one of those chicks at the station who swoons over that rank accent of yours?" Tick swings out of the car door. "I'm getting you two double expressos." Tick emphasizes the 'ex.'

"Espressos. Ess. No 'ex.'" Head down, the professor corrects the student.

Tick bangs the car hood. As Fox raises his head, Tick flips him off.

thirty
late, late night—the fifth day

THE SUSPECT SITS ON A FADED, purple plastic chair with his back to Fox. He faces the mirror separating the interview room from the audio-visual area where Cap and the IT tech, Tyler, sit.

Fox leans against the scuffed beige wall with his long legs crossed in front of him. He's directly behind the suspect. His jacket is off, tie pulled down, playing Brick Breaker. Fifteen minutes into the interview, the older man has yet to participate.

The suspect's face is a pitiful reddish-purple, spreading from the bloody bandage on his nose.

Tick sits opposite the guy at a wooden table, balancing on his chair's back legs. Fox's silence rattles him because it's not silent. His partner's anger vibrates.

"You talk, we might make a deal," Tick reasons. "Breaking and entering, assault on a cop — we can't take some stuff off the list. Attempted kidnapping, mandatory life."

"Youph broke ma nose. Asshault. I'm filing chargshes." The man shuffles in his seat, struggling not to glance behind him.

Tick laughs. "Good luck, buddy. Anyway, I didn't break your nose. I mighta aimed lower."

"Somsh one of you pigsh broke mah nosh."

"Yeah, well, move off for a better subject. Try to focus. You're facing life. Pull your shit together here. Want to go down for somebody else? Really? Your ticket punched on someone else's card? Not me, man. Never."

"Never is shright. I'll be outta here sho fast. Waschh me now, caush I'm already gone."

"How you figure this happens, Einstein? The senator coming to pick you up personally? Sending a private plane?"

The man's eyes dilate, his eyebrows flickering as he works to keep his expression neutral.

"Yeah, man, we all brainless here. Don't know what chuz is about, right?" Tick raises his hands in mock surrender, laughing. He leans in at the perp. "Wise up, stupid. You're trash flying and your supposed savior is the wind."

Cap buzzes. The interruption is unusual.

Fox nods to Tick and walks out of the room. He's gone five minutes, tops. When the detective comes back, he's carrying a creased brown folder. He stands right next to the suspect, almost on top of him. The man twists away in his chair. Fox inches closer.

Tremors race up Tick's neck, but his partner seems calm.

"Tell me about your taste in jewelry, Roscoe. Do you like antiques? Do you like rubies?" Fox's voice is so quiet both men hold their breath.

"Name's not Roshcoe. Don't know about jewree, don't care."

Fox leans further, his mouth a millimeter from the suspect's ear. The man cringes and slides his chair further away. The detective pulls a photo out of the brown file, placing a picture of the weird old lady pin on the table.

"What do you mean, Roscoe? You don't like this? Isn't this special?" Fox winks at Tick. "I think this pin is quite special. Extraordinarily special, as my partner here might say. In several ways. Are you aware Senator Conway wore this pin? I mean, on his person? Or should I say *in* his person?"

In his person?

"Roscoe." Fox brushes his arm against the suspect. "Guess what we found on this pin? All over this pin? Were you aware

Conway lost a cap from his front tooth in the last assault? Where we found this cap?"

The guy is shaking and leans away, but Fox presses on him, forcing the man to glance at the picture. He flinches and forces a harsh laugh, jerking his head away.

Sap is chewing his tongue like it's gum.

Fox leans in further.

The suspect turns directly to Fox and snarls. "Useless asshole. You couldn't stop Con. You couldn't keep anyone safe from me. Been out for almost twelve years! How many little pink ones do you think I've had? Sorry, I missed the glorious Marls. She's dried up by now. You think Con doesn't have the address where you and Grace-bitch sleep?"

In a single motion, Fox grabs the suspect, chair and all. Tick can't jump over the table quickly enough. The detective throws the guy across the room.

Chair and all.

The man crashes into the wall, his head slamming into the corner. He lands tangled in the purple chair, which is broken in two.

Blood splashes on Fox's white shirt, splattering down the front of his suit.

The thug shrieks, clutching himself, cowering, kicking the pieces of faded plastic out into the room.

Tick catches Fox at his waist as he lunges for the guy again. Uniforms rush into the interview room. Three of them wrestle the detective outside.

Damn, Shay. Tick shakes his head. *I couldn't stop him, with five inches and fifty pounds on him. Damn-nation.*

Tick tries to shrink his 6'6" frame into the corner as Cap shifts between reasoning with Fox and threatening him.

"We got the bastard on the pin. We got him on the videotape

at Marley's. Conway will fry this time. Everything's coming together." Cap paces the room, trying to calm his fuming detective. "Look, I let you stay in this case as a favor. Wondering now about the wisest choice, *cywir*? [correct?] This has been an epic night's work, and you try to piss all over everything."

Fox sits, scowling. Silent, impenitent.

"What did he mean about Marley?" Cap leans forward in a warning to his lieutenant. "Who is this asshole?"

The detective howls in rage, throwing his head back. "He's Conway's longtime bodyguard, the same one, years ago in Boston. From my library." Fox tries to stand, but Cap pushes him down.

Fuck. Tension balls Tick's shoulders. *Fuck.*

"Don't you see, Skip?" Fox raves, his fists clenched. "Didn't you listen? Conway put that slime into the kid's camp. Gave his own daughter to be savaged! He planted him to go down when Conway needed a fall guy in his divorce. *Oh, my God, my God, how are people like this allowed to breathe?* We do *not* have him! Clues? We had clues in Boston and *nothing! We have nothing.*"

"*Tawel,*" Cap soothes. "Quiet."

He's out of control.

"The bodyguard will protect him, take another fall. We *do not* have nearly enough, Cap. Not enough."

Tick groans at the bodyguard's stupidity, shocked at the trade-off. The sacrifice of years of life in prison for a snake? *Where do bastards like Conway find with their useful idiots?*

"We won't let him escape, Fox. We've got DNA."

"*Dydych chi ddim yn gwrando.*" [You don't listen.]

"I heard him, Fox. I listened. Go home." Cap murmurs. "Kiss your lovely wife, your wonderful kids. You hear me? Today is over for you."

The senior officer motions to the uniforms. "Take Lieutenant Argall home. Why don't you two go into the house with the good doctor? Stay, have breakfast at the Argalls, stay for lunch, get me?"

He pokes Fox on the nose. "Scram. Don't make me ask these

kids to help you out. *Peidiwch â chodi'ch petticoat ar ôl pissing."* [Don't lift your petticoat after pissing.]

Fox glares at Cap, turns to Tick, and storms out, the uniforms following.

"That shit on tape?" Tick's voice is tight.

Cap smiles. "The senseless smut is fine — got his bell rung a little. You think I earned these bars without knowing my own men?"

The senior officer rubs his face, scrubbing a day's worth of bristle. "Find out what those letter numbers mean, Tick. My gut tells me the letters are a key."

The letters, the smelly letters. Tick wriggles his nose. "I'm on it. The scumbag is what, 200 pounds?"

Cap walks toward the door and turns on his way out. "Oh, hell no. No way. Only 190."

"Wicked damn. Halfway up the wall."

"Watch him, Ticker. The only person who can control Fox Argall is trapped inside his head. We're walking a tightrope with no net."

Tick's head rests on his desk. He's snoring.

Cap leans out of his office and gestures to the nearest deputy. Pointing at Tick, he says, "Give him thirty minutes and trip over his chair."

Twenty minutes later, to the relief of the officer, Tick jerks awake.

The letters. The smelly letters. This stack has nothing except this string of numbers.

Fox's notes contained words. They may have seemed nonsense to some, but Fox said Mac understood them on some level.

These are crazy. Random — they seem random — numbers scrawled in pink ink and not aligned. The odor is disgusting. Tick stares at the digits, allowing them to go out of focus. A trick he learned in the military. Sometimes, when you focus back in, your brain tells you something you haven't noticed. He stares at the notecards again and reaches for his phone, dialing the number for his old navigator.

"Hey, Nick, man. I need you to check out a puzzle for me. Yeah, the time, the time. Almost dawn, damn, you a sleepy puss now? OK, I'm on my way. Put coffee on. Whine, whine, whatever. Be in your kitchen in twenty."

thirty-one
very early morning
—the sixth day

TICK SITS in Nick's wood-paneled kitchen drinking coffee. "Mountain man, don't you feel claustrophobic in this place? It's like a Hobbit House carved out of a tree trunk."

Nick is still in his boxers, hunkered over the smelly letters. "No clues for me, right? Decorating advice is to distract?"

"Honestly, I don't have a clue. I wouldn't give you one if I did, but this time, word, man."

The navigator sighs and yawns. "How do these problems always come at 4 a.m., Ticker?" He doesn't expect an answer. "Well, make me more caffeine."

Walking to the fancy European coffee maker, Tick says, "I will say this, man. Your brew is not like the camp. Or the department. Ours literally stinks. I'm going to sit here in this freaky orange velvet round thing. Ugly as hell, but quite comfortable."

An hour later, Nick shakes the detective awake. "Tick, I think I got this. I think I know what these are. You have more of these?"

"Give me a second." Tick slogs to wake, standing and shaking himself. "What?"

"You got more of these letters?"

"Nine. I got 'em in my bag."

"Let me have them."

Tick unzips his bag and hands the letters to Nick. Despite the plastic sleeves, perfume wafts through the air. His stomach flips, and he has to fight not to vomit.

Nick lays the letters on his table, arranging them by date. After about five minutes of staring and frowning, he rearranges them. "Tick, these are dates and locations."

He leaves the kitchen and comes back with a computer, typing rapidly for a few minutes. Motioning Tick over, he points to the screen. "Mixed elements, arranged like code. See, here's a coordinate, right here. New York City, the coordinates for, say, Times Square, the Marriott Marquis. These numbers are the coordinates. Split them in half, right here? On both sides. At one end, the zip code, and at the other, the area code, and finally a building number. Locations, Tick. Specific locations, exact addresses. These are dates, here. Not the dates on the note, dates embedded in the code. Makes the combination."

Panic shoots up Tick's spine. He points to the last letter on the table.

Nick looks at him. "You OK?"

"What's the date and address on this last one?" Tick chokes. He already knows.

Nick enters the numbers into his computer. "Here. Today. Right here in Jupiter. 128 Sophia Court. The date is today."

The detective gathers the plastic-covered notes and heads out the door, dialing 911. "This is Detective Sergeant John Tickman, Badge 34213. Every available unit to 128 Sophia Court in Abacoa, yes, Lieutenant Argall's. I mean now."

Racing down I95 to the exit at Donald Ross, he heads to Abacoa, past the new Scripps Research building, and turns off his lights. He rolls onto Sophia Court at the back, in the alley; house number 128 is dark. Tick takes his weapon from the holster as he runs to the kitchen door, which is open. As he starts in, he sees a body in the bushes. One of the police officers assigned to protect the Argall family lies dead. His throat sliced from his ear to his clavicle.

Moving into the house, Tick slides along the wall to the

opening of the family room. A person is standing by the hallway leading to the downstairs bedroom. *The master bedroom.* The figure is too dark to identify clearly, but male, and not Esther Diaz, the second uniform assigned to the house. *This man is not a cop.*

thirty-two
dawn—the sixth day

THE HOUSE SITS IN SILENCE. Fox is hanging over the edge of the small sofa at the end of their four-poster master bed, still in his bloody shirt and suit.

Too much of everything.

The relentless pounding of too much. Numbing. The bodyguard got one call, and Fox knows every minute after the call brings the threat to his family closer until Conway is in custody.

Grace is buried under the duvet, halfway down the bed.

The side door from the garage clicks shut. The sound jolts him straight. He cocks his head.

Where did the noise come from? He glances at Grace. She doesn't move. He had insisted on a sleeping pill last night, knowing his wife would never sleep otherwise.

Where are the uniforms assigned outside the house? They are not allowed to enter. They can't come in.

Not a cop.

He's here.

Fox drops to the floor and inches to the door.

Come on, make another noise.

Yes. A light step padding on tiles near the kitchen. He crouches on the floor, waiting for the next noise.

Which way is he going?

The next creak is on the stairs, moving away, toward the second floor. Fox slides out of the bedroom on his belly. His service Glock is in the gun safe below the table at the end of the hallway.

Out in the open.

Why didn't I bring the Glock into the bedroom? He crawls to a small table inside the bedroom door and pulls his Ruger out of a drawer hidden underneath, loading as he shifts back to the door. All he can think of is Grace. Marley. Theiss. Josh.

Sorry, ych fi—mae'n draed moch arna fi. I've made a mess of this.

He slips out, pulling the door closed behind him, flipping the lock. The lock won't hold long, but every second is going to count. Inching down the hall, he gets about a foot from the family room and hears the whispering voice. A familiar chill comes over him. He remembers the recorder in his jacket pocket from his visit with Deacon and clicks the button.

"Ellis." The whispering is louder now. "Ellis Argall. What do they call you now? 'Fox'? How appropriate. Absolutely love. So... manly." Conway steps out of the family room in front of the kitchen to the hallway, an antique 1908 Pistole Parabellum Luger in his hand.

Fifteen feet away. Fox's calculations are rapid. The distance to the bedroom doors, the kitchen, the front of the house.

"Ooh! Look at him, *thinking*. Thinking is what you do best, yes, *Doctor* Argall?" Conway laughs, a trill whinny. "The most overqualified police detective on the planet, quite possibly the universe, wouldn't you say? Some would say you're ridiculous, the ultimate failure... no, not me, of course. But crawling on the floor, *seriously*. Please talk to me, Dr. Argall. Stand like a real man. I'm listening."

Fox waits. Looking at Conway, working out how long he can stall.

Conway leans forward. "I said *stand and speak to me*, Dr. Argall," he hisses.

Fox's back stiffens, but he remains crouched. A smaller target.

"Your front tooth fixed, Conway? You didn't expect the smack in the mouth, did you? Talk of failures. Can't handle your prey? Certainly, you understand this is over for you. The end, right?" Fox emphasizes his accent.

"*Senator* Conway." Conway's face twists. "Oh, your lovely accent... So invigorating."

Conway tries to lighten his voice and fails. "I wouldn't bet against me, Dr. Argall. Oh, right. You did bet against me, and how did you fare?" Shrill laughter echoes in the empty room.

"Your dead friend... some would say mentor." The man waves his arms dramatically. "Was Mac simply a *friend*, Fox? I love to believe he was more. He named you 'Fox,' didn't he? How did your stubborn disrespect help your Mac? *You* created all this."

Conway giggles. "Quite a lovely time, in many ways. Completely enjoyed my time *with you*, of course. I wish you had something to bribe me with, Dr. Argall. All these females. Can't you sire a proper man?"

"Why did you use an IV and not syrup? Weren't sure of the weight? Not enough time for the chip placement?"

"Oh, this is so perfect. I love when you talk *medical*, Dr. Argall. So exciting. I believe we're bonding." Conway snorts a laugh. "Can you believe they were back-ordered on the syrup? So inconvenient. I'm not concerned about the sedation after they're bound."

Conway leans forward and rasps. "A man needs a little *spirit* under him, don't you think, Dr. Argall? *Is your Gracie spirited?* I hate IVs. The last one extravasated and oh... How unpleasant. *Extravasated.* Ah! I can speak medical too."

"Conway, you are made." Fox fights to keep his voice neutral. "Nothing left for you now, no way to sort this. You lost. We both understand why you came here — snuck in here in the middle of the night like the common thug you are. You've lost everything."

"You *took my man*, Dr. Argall. *Snatched him.* I bet you hurt him... you're like me, Ellis. You're violent. You're an animal. You liked hurting him... how much do you like domination, El-lis? I *watch* you. I saw you the first day, in your library. You lifted him off the ground, threw him like he was trash! You're an animal pretending to be human. Kill what gets in your way, yes? We are the same. I admit, coming here, alone, being with you. A *climax*, don't you think? How many have you hurt? How many have you killed? Tell me how you *feel* when you take them fully."

Fox squats in the hallway's darkness, assessing the environment. Without a sound, a shadow closes in behind Conway. Two arms raise into the light streaming in the window from the street, locking Conway in the sight of an outstretched weapon.

A Glock.

Thank God for you, Tick. Fox lowers his body prone and moves his head to miss the bullet path. "Conway," he whispers the name to give his partner his position.

Conway tries to smile, but his face tightens. "*Senator* Conway. *Please.* I've been so polite. Addressed you by your title, your well-earned title, all those hard-earned letters you have trailing after your name? *Get off the floor.* Stand straight like a man."

A toy squeaks in the shadows. Fox groans. *Tick!*

Startled, Conway turns.

Fox vaults into him, knocking the pistol to the ground as he swings the man into the air, yelling, "Got him, Ticker, bring your cuffs."

Conway twists in Fox's grip, pulling out a knife. He lunges, slicing into the detective's chest.

A shot jolts through the quiet as Fox hits the tiles. Blood and brain matter spray over his head and cover his face. A bullet crashes into the wall. Blood splashes on the white-tile floor and bounces, a slow-motion dance into the air.

The acrid smell of gunpowder fills the air, stinging Fox's nostrils as he struggles to regain his footing. His ears ring with the echo of the gunshot, a high-pitched whine that drowns out every other sound. Time slows down as he watches Conway's body crumple to the ground, a trickle of blood seeping from the bullet hole in his forehead. Fox's chest heaves with each ragged breath, his heart pounding against his ribcage as the adrenaline courses through his veins, blurring his vision.

Conway stumbles forward. He thrusts the knife impotently into the air, blood dripping from an exit wound through his forehead. He drops to his knees and falls forward, his face smashing into the tile.

Fox pushes from the floor, slipping in gore and stumbling into the wall. "Tick!"

"Daddy." Marley stands frozen behind the dead man, Fox's service Glock 22 extended in her trembling hands. The sun is rising. Pink and yellow streams flow across Marley's shoulders, down her muscled arms. Her eyes are wide with shock, her face drained of color. A strangled sob escapes her lips as the reality of what she's done sinks in.

"Marls." Fox can barely squeeze her name out. "Marls, lower the weapon, darling girl."

Tick steps out from the kitchen and steadies his weapon at Marley, holding his breath. Sirens scream, and lights bounce off the shadowed walls as police vehicles arrive outside.

"I'm coming to you, Marls. *Dw i'n dod amdanoch chi. Gostwng y gwn.*" [I'm coming for you. Lower the gun.]

Marley slowly lowers the Glock, her body shaking violently. Tears streak her face. "I'm so sorry, Daddy. I'm so sorry."

Anguish contorts Fox's voice. "*Rwy'n dod draw, anifail anwes melys.* I'm coming over, sweet pet. I'm coming for you." He moves to his daughter, taking the gun from her clutching hands, and pulling her into his arms.

"Daddy, Daddy," Marley whispers. "I didn't have a choice. I couldn't throw him out the window. I couldn't find a good plan."

The two sink to the floor. Fox strokes Marley's hair, her face. "*O, fy merch hyfryd, annwyl.* Oh, my lovely, darling girl. You had a good plan. I'm so sorry you had to carry it off."

thirty-three
sunday—it's over

FOX SITS ON THE BED, holding his breath. If he doesn't breathe, he can stop the pain.

Grace stands over him, a mixture of concern and fury on her face. "How much Ambien did you give me, Dr. Argall? How did I sleep through this madness?"

I used triazolam. "A different dose, I admit," Fox says. "But you're quite tiny and you weren't used to a normal dose."

"Different dose."

He doesn't look at his wife. "We weren't going to get through last night without Conway showing here or sending his dogs. Inevitable after we apprehended his bodyguard at Josh and Marley's. I'm obligated to protect you. You wouldn't stay out of the middle if you thought the kids were upstairs."

"So many things are wrong with this decision, Ellis. So many things. I'm not a child you just run over. Protect me? What if I needed to move quickly? What then? You thought he — or someone — was coming. Why did you allow us to stay here?"

"I moved the kids to a hotel after you slept. I would let no one near you. I would die first."

"Yeah, well." Grace glowers, walking into the closet.

Cap skewered Fox when he got to the house and found Grace functionally unconscious. The senior officer called his lieutenant an 'arrogant, self-serving asshole,' accusing him of using his wife. "You need her so viscerally you couldn't face the fucking night without her! You put her in the line of fire. If I can figure a way to write you up for this, I will."

Fox wouldn't mention Cap to Grace.

Exactly the right thing. I'd do the same thing again.

From the closet, Grace calls, "Tick was here when everything happened?"

"Tick was the one who nailed down the date, which was last night. He also figured the location for Conway's ultimate show of crazy. Worked out Conway was headed here. The notes? They were locations. Locations and bragging. He was telling me where he attacked the kids. From the chip info, we were aware he was threatening Theiss."

Fox omits the newer notes with the numbers and the chip threatening Grace. "A mystery, those notes. No one could sort them. We never had this evidence for the trial in Boston or we might have nailed him before all this. Tick interpreted the notes and showed in time to save the day."

Fox will never say everything out loud. Some things go into a deep vault.

"Marley saved the day," Grace says. "Saved our day, anyway."

The doorbell rings and Fox startles awake, grimacing with pain.

"They're here, Lad," Grace calls from the bathroom. "I'll go."

"No, Gracie... *I'm coming!*" Fox pulls a handkerchief from his pocket, wipes his face, and rolls sideways off the bed to avoid at least some of the pain. He makes his way through the family room and opens the door to his partner. *And the beautiful Dalia.*

Grace didn't say Tick was coming, let alone Tick and a date. Life rises, always renewing. He snickers. "Well, hullo, hullo, you two. Lovely you're here, Dalia."

"Thank you, Lieutenant Argall." Dalia blushes.

Tick glares at Fox, motioning with his eyes in a weird way. *What does he want?* Fox can't figure out what he has done — or is supposed to do.

"D, I'm sure you can call the Lieutenant 'Fox.' Everyone does." Tick pats his boss' shoulder.

Fox stutters, nonplussed. "Well, of course, Dalia, of course. We are family here, right? My Christian name is Ellis, but most people call me 'Fox.'"

"Time to go, guys! Make it snappy!" Grace calls from the kitchen. "Fox, will you drive?"

Fox's face falls. "I will if I have to."

"You let me drive because you don't want to?" Tick shakes his head.

Fox's eyebrows rise.

"Uh, Gracie, I always drive." Tick hears himself, shocked. *Damn.* "I meant Grace. I mean Grace."

Grace beams at the big detective. "John Tickman, I would be so proud if you called me Gracie."

Fox scowls. Tick shifts away from his partner's radiating irritation.

"I don't have a nickname, you know? And my husband has so many. Doesn't seem fair, huh, Dalia?" Grace glows as she walks out the door.

Fox motions for Dalia to follow, glaring. Tick takes his date's waist, guiding her back in front of his partner, and bolts to the car.

"You got shotgun, D." Fox tries his cool talk as he slips into the backseat of the car.

Tick catches Dalia's eye and motions, 'he's crazy.' She giggles and gets into the front seat.

"Do either of you have your own church? One you attend regularly?" Grace asks.

"Yes ma'am." Dalia smiles. "Across town."

Grace smiles back, her face glowing. "Well, you'll enjoy this one. Wonderful worship; my daughter, our daughter, Marley, helps her godfather. Tick, you've met Pastor Roofie, haven't you?"

"Don't think so, pet, but he'll remember Miss Marion," Fox interjects. He reaches into his pocket for his phone, opening Brick Breaker.

"Miss Marion? She's my pastor!" Dalia chortles.

Tick's shoulders twitch.

"Too bang on," Fox murmurs. "Right here, Tick, pull over to the left lane."

Music emanates from the church as Tick and Dalia follow the older couple into the narthex. The worship team practices before the service, and the pews are usually full of people who want to experience the music. Roofie is singing 'Amazing Grace.'

The pastor spots Fox and his entourage. He nods to Marley, who accompanies him on piano. He jumps off the stage and heads to the entrance, still singing. Jacob leans out of the pew and hands him a cordless mic.

Roofie's tenor fills the building. He hands Fox the mic and waves for the congregation to encourage the detective, who is red and shaking his head.

"Our song, El," Roofie urges. "Won't you sing with me? Remember, our voices are Christmas presents."

Fox joins his dearest friend, his brother, in harmony for the chorus. The congregation bursts into applause.

"Here's my dad, Lieutenant Fox Argall," Marley calls out as her fingers dance in a flurry over the piano keys. "He's my hero. He taught me to sing and to play the piano, and bunches about life. We start a new beginning today. Daddy, why don't you come here and play with me? Everyone wants to worship with us."

As Fox and Marley's voices blend, the congregation falls silent, transfixed by the raw emotion in their performance. The music swells, offering a sense of hope and renewal. The father and daughter pour their hearts into the song, their shared pain and love evident in every note. As the final chord fades away, the congregation erupts into applause: for the performance, for the solace and strength in the power of music, and for the love of family.

Life is too complicated for some people. Some decide to leave everything. Some survive by demanding their way. The familiar. For others, like Marley, the simplicity shines out from the complexity, allowing an unobstructed view of the best path home. The best way to love.

coming soon! here's a preview of book two: the sweater case

The Sweater Case, Fox Argall Mysteries, Book Two

Prologue

You can lose anything in a Florida swamp. Most think Florida is all cartoon creatures and sunshine. It's more humid overgrowth and genuine creatures that hide in shadowy places.

One — Florida Swamps Are For Keeps

Hobe Sound, Florida

The rain had poured for days.

Joe Cutchens watches water run off the border of his property on Bridge Road, flooding the weed-clogged roadside gulley. The water is already rolling across the busy county road in multiple places.

"Rain is always a blessing here until it's not," Everly Cutchens says. "A river runs through it, Dad."

"Damned ditch is clogged again. The whole thing is useless. Worse than useless. Dangerous," the farmer grouses, pawing at the rain on his face. "And gonna stink to high heaven when we hit ninety degrees tomorrow."

"I'll call in as soon as we get back to the barn." Everly squats at the fence line and points. "Dad, see fifteen feet away to the right, by the road? What is the red thing caught on the branch?"

Joe holds the barbed wire and leans out over the ditch. "A sweater. Like, a knitted thing." He peers closer into the rushing water and says, "Oh, Lord, this may be something."

"Tie yourself off, Dad." Everly wraps a rope at her father's waist and loops it on a post. "I'll throw my weight against you."

"OK, Ev, I'll go slow. Yank me up if I start to slip."

"Eyes open, Dad. Might be gators in here!"

Joe lowers into the muddy trough and wades through the cold, gray-green stream, taking multiple swipes at the red material before stepping on something and sliding sideways. "Damn! Rolled on a can or something," he growls, fighting to right himself. "My whole damn shirt is soaked." He steadies, finally able to drag the dripping blob out. "A sweater, but no one's parts are attached."

"And no gators," Everly adds, grinning.

"No gators." Laughing in relief, he tosses the recovered object to his daughter. "The way it bobbed as it floated. I dunno what I thought. Whatever. Help me crawl back. The side is slick, and I don't want to fall back into this mess."

Martin County Sheriff's Department

"Dammit, Howell, these ditches are a problem! I about drowned getting this thing out of the water at my northeast fence line." Joe Cutchens throws the drenched sweater material on the front desk at the Martin County Sheriff's Office, splattering greenish water.

"Why the hell would you do such a fool-ass thing, Joe?"

Sheriff Howell Farling frowns at his old friend, swiping the algae-flecked water from the counter with his hand.

"I thought it was a kid! You think I wade in gator trenches for fun? We need something done with every drainage ditch on Bridge Road. Overgrown with vines now and not fit for purpose."

"Leave this thing here," Howell sighs. "I'll use the mess as a prop with Geoff when the Palm Beach—Martin Sheriff's Task Force meets later today. Got a couple new members coming from Palm Beach. One's a fancy scientist-turned-cop. Hope to use his juice to punch through some red tape. I'll try to go in sideways with Roads and describe a potential danger."

"There's a *real* danger, Sheriff. Would you step into one of those ditches?"

"Like you, Joe, I'm born and raised. I wouldn't walk in a deep puddle anywhere in Florida. Leave me the mess. Let me work my magic."

The Palm Beach County Sheriff's Department, West Palm Beach, Florida

Captain Skip Harley turns his back on his lieutenant and walks to his perfectly placed orchids.

"Dammit, Fox, I assigned you to this Task Force. You do *not* choose your assignments! Be at the Martin County Sheriff's office at 1 p.m. unless you want to meet the Task Force for lunch at Harry and the Natives. Like this would ever happen. Hear me? The subject is closed. No discussion. Period."

Cap's office is a shining example of OCD, and his prized orchids are the crown jewel. If you show too much interest, the senior officer will throw Latin genera around like leaves falling in the autumn.

Detective Lieutenant Fox Argall sprawls on the green leather chair in front of his boss's desk. His thumbs slide across his phone, the jaunty Brick Breaker tune bebopping in the background. "I'm seriously not the best choice for this. Tick, well, he's nicer than me. They will like Tick, and *voilà*, they will like you. All of which is unlikely with me."

Cap turns to his subordinate. "Well, you're threatening me, Lieutenant Argall. Or should I say, Doctor Argall, as the entire point of you being on this task force is your fucking over-educated background. Tick is a helluva lot nicer than you, but he has no law degree or medical background in molecular genetics. People who don't know you think your brain makes you an asset, even if we understand it is a black-fucking-hole of assholishness."

"Surely not a proper word? American English is still a mystery to me, decades and multiple academic degrees on. I ask myself, is this actually English? A bit like a mixed metaphor, as well." Fox never looks from his game.

Cap understands his lieutenant well—too well. His gaze drifts to the framed photo on his desk, a younger version of himself standing beside an older man with the same piercing blue eyes. "My father always said stubbornness was a *treftadaeth wych Cymru*—a great Welsh heritage. He loved you. The single, solitary reason I haven't kicked your Welsh ass a dozen times in our fifteen years."

"Seventeen years, but you'd probably rather forget the *blinedig* [troublesome] lawyer, straggling behind pestering you."

"A damned *pennbleth*, a massive headache you were. And still, everything remains the same." Cap jabs his finger at Fox. "You will go to the Task meeting and pretend to be a normal human. *Byddwch yn* fucking normal, *am unwaith*." ["Be fucking normal, for once."] He waves his hand at his subordinate, motioning him out.

Fox strolls from his captain's pristine glassed office into the dirt-stained Violent Crimes department as his partner, Sergeant John 'Tick' Tickman, walks in. The lieutenant taps his watch and points to the wall clock.

"7:05 a.m., it is. Ticker, my *consigliere*, my trusted one. Once more, I have finished our morning report with the captain in your absence, consequent to your pathologic tardiness." Fox gestures to the coffee room. "We can grab coffee and discuss our afternoon meeting with the Martin—Palm Beach Task Force. You have been specially chosen to delegate our fine department. Cracking good, you."

Tick shakes his head. "I'm not drinking swill. I'm also dubious of my delegation. Coulda sworn that was you, Boss."

Fox ignores Tick and heads to the door. "Bourgeois swill it is."

Cap yells out the door, "Fox, Ticker. Head to Riviera Beach. They found a body. I'll text the address."

Two — A Better Way to Die

Singer Gardens, Singer Island, Riviera Beach, Florida

Two Riviera Beach police officers stand on the ninth floor of an ocean-side condo, looking down at the expensive rug and avoiding the detectives' eyes. A salty breeze wafts through the open balcony door, carrying the distant sound of crashing waves and the cries of seagulls. Floor-to-ceiling windows flood the room with natural light, showcasing a breathtaking view of the Atlantic Ocean.

Tick shrugs. "Yes, the body is, in truth, a body, and the body is dead. Agreed, not in an expected place, but this alone doesn't make this situation one for Violent Crimes, Sammy."

Sammy's face is etched with uncertainty and embarrassment while his partner shifts his weight from foot to foot.

Tick smiles and pats the young man on the shoulder. "The fact we're cousins doesn't mean you should call my captain whenever you want. Captain Harley?" He motions to Fox, leaning against the entry door frame. "His heart is set on Lieutenant Argall and me staying in our lane. Seriously, guys. This specific body is in his own home and—I dunno, 104 years old or so?"

The second young officer frowns, looking toward the lieutenant. "Sergeant Tickman, this guy is kinda famous. We thought maybe Dr. Argall should check him out."

Sammy nods in agreement.

"Ah, well," Tick agrees, "'kinda famous' is a complication. Naked on the balcony? A brain twister, for sure. But, guys. Not a case for Violent Crimes unless the Medical Examiner decides the crime is violent. You call the M.E.'s office?"

The Riviera cops glance at Fox, who pays no attention to them.

"My partner and I have an important Task Force meeting at noon. Let me call the Medical Examiner. Dr. Argall and I'll hang here if Dr. Gaffley can send someone soon."

The detective raises his eyes to his sergeant and winks.

Tick flips him off behind his back, grinning at the officers. "The examiner's office will straighten all this out."

Like magic, Chief Medical Examiner Ez Gaffley appears and strolls past Fox into the condo apartment.

Tick exhales and chuckles. "See, boys? He's here to answer all the questions. You got a new psychic transport system, Doc? I mentioned you, like, two minutes ago. How did you find us so fast? We got a naked dead guy."

"Dr. Argall called me ten minutes ago. Said 'naked with bourbon.' Sounds interesting. I was driving by and thought I'd take a gander. Wassup?"

The medical examiner is an example of how to live life well. He's easy-going until you cross him, and you're on your butt. He assesses the room and jerks a thumb at Fox, who hasn't acknowledged the chief except to move out of his way. "Your partner have any opinions?"

"He's always got opinions but doesn't always share with the class. You tell us what's up, Doc." Tick rolls his eyes and flicks his hand at the naked, elderly man, feet covered in bright yellow socks, sitting on a chaise on his balcony. A glass of bourbon sits on the table beside the body.

"Doctor Argall. Want to assist me? I'll make you a deputy medical examiner. Add to your curriculum vitae." Ez walks to the balcony. "A mystery, yes? You like mysteries."

Fox audibly groans but pulls himself away from his game. "Not likely a mystery. Clear cardiac arrest. You'll find nothing to exert yourself here. This boy went out exactly as he dreamt. Bang on, I'd say. Here are the bikinis at the Hilton below and the rich, caramel scent of the best bourbon." He points to the bottle of Blanton's bourbon on the floor beside the naked guy and peers theatrically over the side of the balcony toward the hotel.

"So, you simply called to enjoy my company?" Ez motions for the local cops to move away, and he squats next to the body.

"Our desire for your company, certainly, plus Florida state law requiring clearance from your office for any unexplained death. The gentleman left his will over here." Fox lifts a piece of paper from a shiny, dark wood side table and reads: "'I, Reginald Carrow, wish to be buried at sea.' One choice for the death certificate. Or 'death unattended.' Your pick."

"Thanks for letting me choose."

"We can jump on the sea burial, as we're right here at the beautiful Atlantic Ocean, to fulfill his last wish."

The Riviera cops appear worried, but Ez pats Sammy as he walks around the body. "No sea burials today, my friends. I'm certain Dr. Argall is correct about the cause of death. But let's examine everything anyway, yes?"

The medical examiner motions for his photographer. "Please document the scene. Game at the Argall house Sunday, *compadre*?"

Ez Gaffley is happily married but kind of in love with Grace Argall, Fox's wife. The relationship is entirely about food. "Grace mentioned *picadillo. Ropa vieja.* 'Better than *la piquera.*' Quite a claim." He finishes with the body and pulls off his gloves.

"Absolutely," Fox mumbles from the door. "You must appear as commanded and keep my lovely wife happy, *o si no, verás.* [otherwise, you'll see [consequences]]. Tick and I are off. Some naff meetings. Later, *asere*."

Ez swings his finger to the door and pats the worried beat cop on the shoulder again. "Let's move the body to my place. Death takes us all, and I'm paid to be suspicious. However, I agree with my colleague. This appears to be a marvelous way to go."

Three — Wildly Disinterested Is More Like It

Martin County Sheriff's Department

"Cap's gonna be pissed I let you talk me into this." Tick walks a step in front of Fox as they arrive at the Martin County Sheriff's Department.

"Nah. Cap understands networking is not my forte. You're my subordinate, Ticker. I order you to come and be my wingman. In fact, my frontman. Thus, you're off the hook."

"I'm your freaking babysitter, Shay," Tick laughs. "I'm never off the hook."

Tick often calls Fox 'Shay,' which is short for Seamus, an Irish name. The first time he called Fox 'Seamus,' he had timed the jibe perfectly for a rare Fox conniption. His Welshman partner went on forever about where Ireland was, how Ireland isn't Wales, and something derogatory about American ignorance. *Still makes me laugh.* "Cap might hit me if I used 'he ordered me' as an excuse."

"Well." Fox's go-to phrase when he's irritated or done talking. He's rarely irritated and often done talking.

Shoving Fox, Tick says, "Ah, what the hell-o, I'll back your play at these meetings. I got nothing better. Unless Cap calls. He calls, and I'm absolutely making background noises like I'm in the loo at the station. Swoosh, right?"

"Lovely job on not cursing and crikey, using 'loo,' bravo," Fox chuckles. "Better job on 'backing my play.' You won't regret the stand."

Tick groans. "Sounds like a foreshadow in a mystery thriller. The ones that never end well?"

Pulling open the Martin County Sheriff's office door, the air conditioning slaps into Tick as it battles the damp heat. *Cold, musty air, old coffee, and anxious sweat stench, in that order.* He smiles at the desk officer. "Hey, man, where do we go for the county Task Force meeting?"

The deputy points behind them at the door. "They're coming in behind you from lunch now."

The door slides open, and the muggy Florida heat pushes back in. Five men and a woman fill the small entry.

Tick thrusts his hand out to the nearest person, the woman. "I'm Sergeant John Tickman from Violent Crimes out of Palm Beach. We're here for the Task Force."

"I'm Deputy Ann Carley, Martin County. This is our team. Are you the full crew from PB?" Flat vowels and clipped consonants scream a rare native Floridian.

"You sound like you're from here. I'm from Riviera Beach." Tick turns to find Fox, who is nowhere to be seen. "Uh, Lieutenant Argall was here a minute ago."

"I think he's down here," The desk officer says. "Are you Lieutenant Argall, uh... Sir?"

Fox is squatting on the floor behind the front desk, staring intently at a piece of fabric in a wire cabinet. "Where did this material come from?"

"Well, that one's no Florida accent." Howell Farling, the sheriff for Martin county, walks over and peers down at the detective. "You must be Dr. Argall. That material came in this morning from a farmer. Farm off Bridge Road. He found it in a run-off ditch."

"Where on Bridge Road?" Fox asks. "Where's the farm located?"

"His property runs to Hobe Sound, bounded by Jonathan Dickinson State Park and I95. He's got some land across the interstate, but they found this nearer to Hobe Sound. Mind sharing your thoughts?" Howell waves his hand to the group.

The detective startles, noticing the gathering for the first time. "Fox. I'm Fox, of course," he says, missing the cue to explain his focus on the red material.

Tick sighs. "I'm Lieutenant Argall's social director. Yes, this is Dr. Ellis Argall. He goes by 'Fox' to most people. We will take this interaction as a harmless warning. Dr. Argall will go off on tangents and struggle to care about what many other people might think of as important. Like Task Force meetings."

"Crikey, Ticker. Harsh." Fox pushes his Welsh accent and throws a dazzling smile at the group. The group visibly relaxes, and Howell smiles.

"Oh, for fuck's sake," Tick mumbles.

Fox glances at his partner but says, "Of course, I'm assigned to this Task Force in part because I have academic backgrounds in medicine and law."

"Dr. Argall is being humble." Howell Farling starts.

"Freaking unlikely," Tick interrupts. "He's too focused on the red thing to bother."

"Well, Ticker, yes." Fox nods. "You have a point—an important point. Here's the real question: Do you have a pair of gloves and a bag sized for this? This is evidence." He points at the material, looking at his partner.

Sheriff Farling motions to the desk clerk, but Ann Carley leans over and hands Fox the gloves and bag.

"Dr. Argall, can you explain your thinking to us?" Ann asks.

"This is a piece of a sweater. I think a woman's, but now children are dressed more maturely—" Fox frowns. "Well, possibly a child's."

"A child's sweater? Looks like a muss of mangled yarn to me." Howell smiles, his eyes twinkling.

Fox takes too long with the gloves, messing with the fingers. Finally, he gives up, smiling at the group watching him. Folding a glove in half, he protects two fingers to put the material in the bag. Lifting the bag to the light, he juggles it gently to move the yarn. "A wide weave with a large yarn width, yes? This section is red, but with a lot of white strings—also yarn? We don't know yet."

"Might be added string," the deputy at the desk muses. "My mom added string to her yarn to strengthen the material. Y'know, so when she washed it?"

"It would hold its shape, yeah?" Fox tilts his head and indicates a small area of woven yarn near the right corner of the bag. "Right here, between these strands? This is blood. Human? Maybe. Yet, here is our problem. This brown stain? I think we have liquid methamphetamine. It has an unusual odor—kinda like fingernail polish mixed with feline urine."

Howell works hard to stop from rolling his eyes. "The thing was floating in a gulley of run-off water. Meth is highly soluble. The yarn is red, for God's sake. How are you so sure about the blood?"

"The blood is actually coffee-ground consistency mixed with other vomitus." Fox shrugs. "Might be wrong, of course. Better safe. I suspect this material floated quite readily, and the open weave of water-resistant yarn may have helped us here. We will find out. Let's consider forensics."

Ann motions the group into a room down the hall. "As everyone describes, Dr. Argall is wildly over-educated. A PhD in Molecular Genetics, an active Medical Degree, and an active—meaning he can practice here—law license. We shouldn't neglect the bonus PhD in criminology, should we?" Ann guides Fox to a chair, but she smiles at Tick. The smile doesn't make it to her brown eyes.

Tick groans. *Jealousy, shit, all we need is someone who thinks they need to compete with Fox.* This macho reaction is expected in some men, but he can't remember envy in a woman.

Women all swoon at Fox. Tick is forced to admit his partner is what anyone would call handsome. He turns on his accent and charm and usually stops—or starts—all kinds of problems.

"Hey, guys," Tick says. "We're never sure when my partner is right, but we accept it's mostly always. At Palm Beach, we've just learned to roll with him. Now. Do we talk about what the new evidence might mean, or should we put the sweater case on the shelf and start Task Force stuff?"

I always take charge of interactions. Except with Cap, who has known Fox for decades. Tick tries to hide when those two scuffle, which is too often for Tick's post-traumatic hyper-vigilance. *Cap is gonna be so pissed.*

Howell moves to the whiteboard. "Let's start the Task Force meeting and send this to forensics. No need to chew on unknowns."

Fox is playing Brick Breaker and doesn't raise his head. "Let's bring Charlie in, Tick. She's the best. County politics aren't a problem; Martin sends their forensics out to Palm Beach. No toes cramped."

"We can hear you." Howell grins. The sheriff appears genuinely friendly.

Smiling vaguely, Fox doesn't respond.

Tick sighs. *He has no idea who's talking. There's no malice in Sheriff Howell.* His eyes shift to Ann Carley. *She's a different story.*

⸻

Be sure to look for all the books in the Fox Argall Mysteries series.

acknowledgments

I'd like to thank a number of people for humoring my creative journey. First of all, my family, who have supported me in all. Thanks to Robyn and Nora Stoy for endless listening and feedback.

Thanks to Mariah Sinclair and Beth Foxcroft for the cover art.

This series was published originally on Kindle Vella.

about the author

Collings MacCrae is the author of murder mysteries.

The Ruin of the Watcher is the prequel to Fox Argall Mysteries. The books are numbered so the reader can fully appreciate the details of the friendships and failures as they develop, although the books are standalone mysteries and can be read in any order. *The Ruin of the Watcher* introduces the main cast of characters and their beginnings from the earliest days of their relationships in Columbus, Ohio, as young adults. Each subsequent book brings a different murder mystery, always with the main cast, and adds interesting new characters along the way.

The list of Fox Argall Mysteries as of this March 2024 printing:

Book 1: The Ruin of the Watcher
Book 2: The Sweater Case
Book 3: The Case of the Reluctant Whistleblower
Book 4: Resurrection of the Ruby Skull
Book 5: Mad Dog Elegy
Book 6: Indecent Ink
Book 7: The Bio-Fake of Bronze John
Book 8: The Rift of Lions

Find them on my Linktree!
https://linktr.ee/CollingsMacCrae
Stay tuned to @Collings_MacCrae on Instagram and @CollingsMacCrae on Twitter and Facebook.

also by collings maccrae

Check out my website at https://collingsmaccrae.com

COMING SOON to e-book and print:

Book 2: The Sweater Case (available on Vella, e-book and print

Book 3: The Case of the Reluctant Whistleblower (available on Vella)

Book 4: Resurrection of the Ruby Skull (available on Vella)

Book 5: Mad Dog Elegy (available on Vella)

Book 6: Indecent Ink (available on Vella)

Book 7: The Bio-Fake of Bronze John (available on Vella)

Book 8: Rift of Lions (in progress; watch me write this book on Vella!)

Made in United States
Orlando, FL
24 April 2024